What Follows

What Follows

Edited by April Steenburgh and C. Lennox

Contents

Introduction   **1**

The White Sisters by Sarah Lyn Eaton3

Monster Godmother by Lyn Thorne-Alder   **22**

Small Victories by E.V. O'Day   **38**

Vindication by Nina Waters   **62**

Walkabout by Joyce Chng   **79**

Extant by Crystal Sarakas   **95**

Ice and Fire by M.J. King   **108**

The 13th Four-Leaf Clover by K Orion Fray   **117**

From Stone to Sky by Ross Bennett   **128**

Silver Linings by Kate Larking   **139**

The Shape of Things by April Steenburgh   **155**

About the Authors   **167**

About the Editors   **171**

Introduction

C. Lennox

As humans, mortality is a heavy subject. Contemplating death for the majority of us is hard to do. We don't like to consider ourselves vulnerable; that one wrong move or one small thing could shuffle us off the mortal coil at any given moment. It's a daunting thought.

So what happens when we expand that concept from the individual and encompass the whole human race? The whole world?

The apocalypse is not a new idea. There have been countless books, stories, movies, and other forms of entertainment centered around the destruction of the human race or this beautiful little mud ball we live on. Hell, even religion has a space in its teachings for how we're going to snuff out of existence.

So why, if we're so hung up on our own dwindling existence, does the idea of an apocalypse not send us into writhing fits of anxiety? I think part of it has to do with the fact that something on a global scale seems far away and almost impossible. The entertainment industry has also used this as a plot vehicle for years, desensitizing audiences to the idea as well.

Some just like to sit around and think of how many ways humanity can kick the bucket.

For *What Follows*, we decided to turn apocalyptic thinking on its ear, and consider it from someone else's point of view. Not humanity, but those that share the earth with those crazy humans. These races, decidedly much longer lived than we, don't have that mortality hang up that we do. So how would those people react to the apocalypse crashing down around their (in some cases, pointed) ears?

We love the idea of letting authors take a small idea and *running* with it, so we purposefully made the anthology theme vague. We like to see what comes back, and boy, we were not disappointed. To see eleven different interpretations of how the world ends and how these different peoples react to it was a treat, and no two stories in this book are the same as a result. We hope that people have as much fun reading it as we did editing it.

We'd like to thank Ruth Stuart, Laura Lee Intscher, and the rest of our Indigogo supporters for showing support in this book early on, helping us get it off the ground. We would also like to thank our loyal readers for being patient with us: it took us longer than usual to pull this book together. This year was fraught with health issues and the death of dear family members. Knowing you were supporting us helped keep us going, and we were able to find solace in working on this book. Thank you.

Now go enjoy the end of the world.

-C. Lennox

The White Sisters

Sarah Lyn Eaton

I was asleep when the world changed. Six of us woke, disoriented and confused. My eldest sister, who had been on watch, was dead, and with her any knowledge of what occurred, leaving a sudden gap in a collective, remembered history that spanned centuries. The forest around us had lost its pigmentation in the absence of a firm sun. In the days that followed, we discovered the entire world had suffered the same.

I understood the shifting greylight enough to know it was late afternoon as we knelt on the ground. My pale hands broke from their finished work and I sat back, shaking the dirt off. This was the richest soil we had found in weeks but it was still too dusty across my skin. I flexed the unfamiliar fingers, watching flesh stretch and bend over sharp knuckles.

Where do we go now, Sister? I heard the voice, and waited for one of the others to reply, tracing sigils of safe passage in the dirt with a slate stone. A hand squeezed my forearm gently and I looked up to see Rowan staring at me, in concern, with honey eyes that mirrored mine. She stood beside me, wrapped in the tattered and threadbare remnants of clothing found discarded in an empty store weeks, maybe months ago. We had been walking for so long it was hard to tell. We dressed to cover as much skin as possible.

Always, I had been surrounded by Sisters, always falling decidedly in the middle. The feel of air on all sides of me sent a shudder through my frail bones. I looked around at the sad trees still rooted in the ground, struggling for life.

I will go where you go, I shrugged. My eyes were on the fresh mound of dirt at our feet. I was the only sister Rowan had left. I stared at the dirt embedded in the prints of my fingertips, like dark grain. Had I water for tears, I would have wept them.

Rowan held her hand out, one that could have been my own, we were so similar in form. We might have been twins if not for the longer slant to her eyes and the elongated fingers and toes of her limbs. Like mine, her hair was hidden out of sight beneath strips of fabric we had wound around our heads. We could shift into human skin, but something of our true nature remained. Our hair gave us away.

I took my sister's hand and she helped me stand. We were unsteady on our feet but we were still moving. We were hardwood. Not many of our kind could bear to abandon their birth groves to become a Sister of Birch. When we did, we took our heartwood as our name within the order.

Sister Rowan's lips were cracked and near bleeding, just as Sister Hazel's had been as she gasped for her last breaths that morning. I knew that if we did not find water soon, we wouldn't be far behind our sister. Rowan brought some of the earth on her fingers to her lips and tasted it. She shook her head sadly. For all of our knowledge, we could find little life left in the world to draw our magic from. Even if we had found more water, we would not have used it. What life was left in the forest we would not sacrifice to sustain our own. I was haunted by the sound of falling trees where there should have been squirrels scuttling and songbirds of all kinds. We of the wild must fight for what life we can.

Rowan was staring ahead. I looked at her, tracing the outlines of her in my memory in case she should suddenly disappear as well. Even frail and covered in dirt we were luminous, so I rubbed some more dirt across my face and arms, where they tucked into my borrowed sleeves. We were too bright in this grey world.

Which way would you choose? Rowan asked. I pointed at the horizon beyond without looking. Through the brush and trees was a rise of earth in the distance. Rowan frowned. *I do not remember that mountain.*

It was not a mountain when last we were here, I answered. Then, much of the exposed earth had been underwater.

We had been walking, rolling backwards through the skins of our own lives, hoping to find others doing the same. Here was another place, remembered in my blood and bone. The journey had cost us so much and taken so long and there was still much more ground to cover. Nothing was as we remembered. The only sounds in the forests were our footsteps. I didn't know how many more we had in us.

A snap in the woods spun us around. Rowan pushed me behind her before I could register the hammering of my heart. A dark man stepped into view. He was lean and wiry, dressed in mended clothes, with a bag slung over his shoulder. I couldn't see any weapons but I didn't doubt he wore one.

"There's traps up the path there," the dark man said, his teeth flashing white against his lips. His voice hung low and smoky in the air, offered words to wounded animals. My sister moved her lips but, long-unused, her words found no purchase in the air.

I don't trust him, she said to me. The man moved, slow, and loosened a clay carafe from his belt. He handed it to her. "Slow sips. Just wet your lips and suck on 'em. You don't want to get sicker." She stared at him. I could smell the moisture of the clay as I reached for it. Rowan pushed my hands away.

The man nodded and put it to his own lips first. He offered it again and Rowan took it and did as he suggested. She passed it to me. I pressed my lips to the opening and felt the water pass over my dry flesh. I sucked on my lips gratefully, drinking in this body's need. I handed it back to my sister.

The dark man pointed to the fresh mound. "You lost someone?" I nodded. He looked us up and down. "You headin' for City, I can get you in. I'm a cyote. My people been ferrymen since the city went up. A family of cyotes." He smiled sincerely, but I couldn't smell coyote in him at all. Rowan turned to me.

I don't trust him, my sister repeated. I touched my damp lips with still shaky fingers.

If this City stands between us and the mountain, it is where we need to go, I sighed. *We don't have a choice.*

"You sure you want in?" the man asked, eyeing me specifically. I nodded and he shrugged. "Not many places left to

go otherwise, I s'pose. Stay behind me. Keep your heads down."
He frowned at us, throwing in an afterthought, "Don't act new."

He led us away from the obvious path and we followed
him silently into the trees. My feet were hardened against the
drying earth and I could no longer feel the stabbing pains of the
rocks and sticks underfoot. Every now and then the stranger
stopped to make sure we followed. The way he regarded us set
me on edge. No matter what skin we wore, there was a spark of
fire within us. Some men could see it. I should have been able to
feel it humming inside me like a hive of wasps, a comforting
vibration. It's the taproot we use to feed on magic, to hold a foot
in each world. The longer we walked, the fainter the thrum
became. I no longer believed there was magic left in the world.
Every day we walked, the light within me grew dimmer.

The dark man stopped at the crest of the ridge. I looked
down and saw the new forest we would have to brave to keep
going. Rowan gripped my hand tightly as the scar on my thigh
twitched nervously, a wound inherited from the last skin I wore.
Dwellings of men stretched out as far as the eye could see in a
basin that had once been populated by fish and crab, a body of
water that had been one of five sisters. We had lived here once, a
stand of white upon the shore. I had memory of glassy blue
waves with frothy, roiling whitecaps. I shut my human eyes tight,
and could almost taste that sun on my face. It was blinding in my
memory.

I opened them to take in the ramshackle city. The cobbled
structures and huts were old and in bad need of repair, many in
states of purposeful dismantling, using the support of the ones
around it to remain upright. To my eyes, the homes were better
the further into City you looked, tree rings of time revealing its
unwritten history and migration. It all seemed to end at a high
wall, leaving no clue as to what lay beyond it.

At the base of the ridge, I could see where acres had been
cleared, where more trees were in the process of being removed.
The trees around us had life in them but their days were already
numbered. We slowly made our way down into the basin by a
path seemingly worn down by time. Several times the man before
us stopped and we followed suit. At the base, I looked up to find

the path had cleverly disappeared. We passed furrowed rows of earth before plunging into the outer alleys of the city. The sudden smell of garbage and time was overwhelming after such an absence of life, and yet... There was another scent beneath the human one. I was sure that City had grown towards the retreating water that I could smell on the air.

***

At the outskirts of the city, in the shadow of our cyote, we drew little attention. We crossed into a nicer area. Almost hidden behind a half wall, a young kid with hard eyes had a bead on us, but still, the others tended to their evening activities, nodding a greeting here and there to the dark man.

He stopped in front of a recycled metal door attached to a small tin hovel and ushered us inside, closing and bolting the door behind him. There was a small cook stove and a well-tended bedroll in one corner and a cistern inside the door. The rest of his place was full of salvaged things. As our host threw some dried patties onto the stove, I wandered about his inventory. My sister planted herself at the outer window, where she could keep watch on our host, as well as the world outside.

There were pots and mirrors on a plank in the corner. Along the wall sat old pieces of mechanics. Clothes with once-bright patterns were tacked to the wall in decoration. I stopped at a pile of weathered and cracked books, sitting on a shelf made of old signs that once hung above the roads that stretched for miles. I caressed the books gently. I could taste the paper with my touch; hue of pine, beech, and even birch. The bones of our children. Something of them remained. I picked the book up and held it to my chest, thinking of the others who had fallen. The man smiled the first smile I had seen on him.

"Those are books. You know books?"

"Yes."

"Gam said people used to read them but no one reads no more. Now we tell stories to each other. That's my job, too. Keeping stories. Those books, they burned them for fuel until there was hardly any left. I save them when I find them. It's what we cyotes do. I got a storage box full of 'em, out of sight. My gam used to say that there were homes just for all of them to live in, just for the books. If true, they must have been the first homes to die, right? Giant blazes to keep the people warm. You check me? You understand me fine?" I nodded. "Maybe that's how all this started," he said with a grand flourish of his arm.

A blaze lit in the stove and the warmth felt good on my skin. Still, the orange flame frightened me. I had seen such devastation wrought by its tongue. I never understood how men could live beside it with such ease. Once the fire in the stove was going, the cyote poured water from the cistern into a cup. My hands started to tremble at the sound of it splashing into the clay vessel. He added some powders from a tin on a high wall and mashed it around with a thick stick. He brought the jar of water over and handed it to me.

"Small sips. Like before. Very tiny." I lifted the clay but relinquished it to Rowan when she put her hand out. She took a bit of water in and hesitated, before giving it back to me. I took it eagerly. My head cleared with every sip, flashing through my entire body in waves. Rowan and I shared it slowly between us. When the cup was empty, I handed it back gratefully. "I am called Mica." He was thin, like the other people we had seen, but he was deceptively muscled. There was some peppering to his hair, but I could not gauge his age.

"Mica," Rowan barked out his name, choking on her own voice. The sound of her in the room startled me. Our host gave her his undivided attention. She pointed to the room and then him. "You are alone?" Mica nodded.

"Just me," he pointed to his chest. He pulled some kind of bright red tuber out of a box behind the cistern and sliced off three pieces. He put one in his mouth and sucked on it, handing another to my sister.

"Suck on it until it is soft enough to chew." He gave me the third piece and I set it on my tongue. It did not have a terribly strong flavor. I waited until Rowan began to chew to take my first bite. It was slightly gritty in my mouth. I could not remember the last time we had found food to eat. Chewing was strange. The tuber tasted like underbrush and heavy starch, but my body seemed to brighten.

"Thank you," I whispered hoarsely, rolling the words on my stiff tongue. He nodded.

"You cyote for these things?" Rowan asked, looking around the room.

"Yes," Mica smiled, his teeth flashing. He was looking again at my weathered jacket with the strange patches embroidered at the shoulders. I shifted uncomfortably under his gaze. He smiled again, in apology. "So. Business. You looking for work?"

"No," Rowan said. "We are not staying."

"Good," Mica nodded thoughtfully. "Where do you go?"

"The other side of the water," I said.

"There is nothing there," Mica frowned. "People came from there long ago. Not in generations."

"Good," Rowan snapped as I yawned. With a bit of food in my belly I suddenly felt how tired I was. Mica was staring at me.

"You think you're safe because you found people. You are not safe here, not you. Not hiding in those skins. We leave tomorrow." Rowan's eyes flashed darkly. My heart was pounding again. I had heard what he said, too.

"Why not now?" Rowan began to collect herself, reaching for me.

"Rest. Eat. Drink. Replenish. It's too late. Not safe at night." He went to the cistern to get more water and powdered herbs for us.

"Why not?"

"The way to the water is only passable in daylight. There are some who do not care to try to farm the salted earth. They guard the way well, to take in trade." He handed me a second cup of his precious water.

He is trying to keep us here, my sister stiffened. I did not sense malice and shook my head. I thought of our other Sister, the one who did not wake me for my turn at watch. We found her half-shifted in her tree skin, turned away from the world. What had she seen that made her choose such a horror? The sorrow made me bone-weary.

Rest sister, I begged Rowan, touching the back of her hand.

Do you trust him? she asked me, watching Mica as he bustled about. *This human?* There was a lilt to her question that made me turn to look at her. *I know of your deal with Sister Oak. I know she used to wake you early. That you used to walk among the people, before it was your turn to watch.*

I blushed horribly and turned away from her. It wasn't forbidden. It just wasn't done. We weren't supposed to want to. We were watchers. It felt important to me, though, to understand the creatures we shared our world with. When the blush faded, I realized she really was asking my opinion. I shrugged. *Like with all creatures, I trust him until I don't.*

Mica's hungry face stared at the object beneath my hands. I was still holding the beloved book on my lap. I could feel that the cover of this book had been stroked often, worn to smooth silk in the center with roughened edges.

"You read?" I asked.

"No," he choked out. "Can you? Read it to me?"

I opened the cover and found words crawled across the front in thick strokes. I could feel Rowan's eyes on me. My hands trembled. Mica sat before me eagerly. "This book belongs to Maggie Riddle." Our new friend waited for more but my voice started to tremble as well. Beneath the large script was a smaller one, faint and splotched, but I could feel the impression of the words in the paper. *For the nights beneath the oak tree, and the star we wished upon together. For an eternity of happiness. I love you.*

"You know books," he spoke in awe.

"I know books."

"Is that all it says?" he asked. I repeated the words, tracing them with my finger. He pointed at the words beneath it but I shrugged.

"I cannot read them. The print is too faint," I lied. I handed him the book and he traced the words as well, mouthing what I had spoken. I knew the words I did not tell him. Eternity was a hard one. Life would alter and change. Maggie Riddle and the one who loved her had learned that, or so the tear stains told me. In such a world what could eternity mean?

"My gam left me this one. Cyotes been passing it down from cyote to cyote." His eyes were sparkling with tears. "Thank you."

"It's a book on healing," I offered, recognizing the letters on the title page. Mica had a scar along his hairline on the left side. It was old and had been expertly tended. The rough scar on my left thigh twinged. When I woke from my last slumber, I found a thick arrow carved into my flesh, below my hip. I had lovingly traced its twin on the birch bark of my companion, fallen on the forest floor beside me. My other skin had expelled me before its end, but I bore the mark carved into us when we were one. The scar hurt, as if it were still knitting itself back together. With that discomfort came a pleasant memory of my smooth, paper skin, like the pages of the book.

"Herbs, my gam said. Most haven't been seen in our time. She said there was a great fire. Many died. And then the sky blackened. The world been growing colder since. I say the sky is brighter than when I was a boy. I say the world is righting itself. But how many will be left when it does? Maybe none of us. Maybe none of you," the dark man was sad.

"We are no different than you," I insisted but he barked out a laugh, long unused.

"You are the meaning of different. I am honored to help."

"What do you think we are?"

He whispered. "Few but me would know it in the world. I believe my eyes and you are not men." I stared curiously as he dropped a hand onto my skin in awe. "Poreless."

"Yet it is flesh, I assure you," Rowan said hotly from the wall. "Same as mine."

"But not mine," he laughed. Tears formed in his eyes and he sat back hard on his feet. "Wonderful. I know you," he said. "More like you come before. They get caught in the traps. None like you come here for a long time. Wasn't sure there were more." Mica jumped up and moved to the corner, digging into a pile. He came over and offered us each a blanket, his hands open. "It's all I have."

"It is more than enough," I answered.

He glanced between me and my sister. "How old are you?"

I tilted my head, in thought for a moment. "I have had many skins," I said. Mica frowned in confusion.

"It is our Order," Rowan explained, choosing to trust him. "When our tree skin nears death, we slip from it and join with a sprout. We are Sisters of the Birch. We are watchers. We witness. We do not interfere." In my heart, I heard many voices speaking in unison.

"We were seven," I said flatly. "The others are lost now."

Mica nodded thoughtfully. "I am the last of my line. As you are the last of yours."

"You could not know that!" Rowan snapped, angry.

"Others have come through," Mica frowned. "Others of magic. All have disappeared."

"They have moved on," my sister snorted. "They would care not for this rambling city of men."

"I would like to believe that," Mica admitted. "But in your travels, your days coming here, did you find others of your kind?" I could feel his heart. He believed his words were true. My sister could, too. She turned away from him. "You may be the last two."

"Of our kind?" I asked sadly, thinking back to the sounds of the falling trees.

"Of all them that are like you, more earth than bone, more tree and stone and water and ether… of all them, you may be the last." Mica stood and turned off the stove, lighting a low candle. I couldn't bear for it to be true, but on our journey we had not found others. We had lost our own. I knew we could well be the last.

Maybe here, Rowan said heavily, *but surely not everywhere. There were many Orders scattered about. Have courage.* She reached over and squeezed my hand. But I had known her for a long time. She did not trust the words she shared.

"When was the last time you saw one of our kind?"

Mica thought on my question. "I did not have grey hair yet and my hands had not finished growing. My gam and my dad were both alive. And my sisters. So, long ago. A man came to town. He was of you."

"Was he like us?"

"No," Mica shook his head. "He was black as soot. Blacker than me. With soft eyes like a flower."

"What was he?" I had never seen such a creature, in all my lives.

"I do not know. Some said he was a dragon. Some said he was from beneath the earth. It did not matter. He was not here long."

There was a knock on the door. Mica's eyes looked to us as he touched a finger to his lips. I pulled the blanket up and turned my head away, feigning sleep. Mica put a hand on the bar across the door before he opened it. Out of the corner of my eye, I spied the small child, with the hard eyes, I had seen earlier. She threw off her hood, exposing a shaved head.

"What can I do for you, Kat?"

"Was wondering what I might do for you, Teach", she peered around him, but we were stilled in shadow, "specifically your new friends I seen."

"What friends would that be?"

"Ones I saw you sneak into town."

"Don't miss much do ya?"

"Not if I wanna make a living, Teach. You know that."

"What were you thinking?" Mica steeled himself against her but she pushed past him into the hovel. Rowan stood to meet her.

"You're new in town," Kat said with authority. "Got a guide yet?"

"Guide?" my sister asked, looking to Mica. The girl sat herself on a crate beside Rowan, pulling her down as if they were best friends.

"There's places in City to be avoided, see? Only City was built to funnel you right into them. Like a trap," Kat's eyes narrowed at us before she broke into a smile. "I can take you where you need to be, safe."

"They're not staying," Mica said firmly. Kat's eyes shifted and she eyeballed him instead, standing, done with us now.

"Seems like you need my help then," her voice was low and even but even I could smell the threat behind it. "Seems some would pay good water for information on new folk." This smile was wide and sharp.

"What are we talking?" Mica was considering the threat as if it were a practiced form.

"You know what I want."

"It's not for trade."

Kat looked at us and back to Mica. "You sure, Teach?" He looked at us hard, and nodded to her, eyes closed. "That's too bad. Sure wish we could have worked something out."

"You come into my place and push business on me. That's not how we do things." Mica's words held blades at their tips.

"Times are hard. Not many in-comers. Native folk get restless and it becomes my problem. Your problem, too." She hesitated in the doorway. "You're a good friend. I'll give you an hour. No deal, no secret."

"Anyone see you sniffing round here?"

"Anyone ever?" And with that she was gone. Mica seemed to come unhinged, pacing and fretting, fumbling through his belongings.

"Mica?" I poked him. He stopped and shook his head.

"Seems we need to meet the dark. Now."

"You said it wasn't safe," Rowan frowned. "She's only a child-"

"And you seem scarcely older. Her teeth are sharp." He became desperately hopeful. "If we could hide you?"

"Without the trees, we cannot shapeshift," Rowan spun sadly. "We are trapped in these bodies." I nodded.

Mica set his lips firm in displeasure. "Then we leave." I rose to my feet as he threw some tubers and books in his bag. He reached for the book I held, slipping it reverently into the bag. He refilled his water at the door and gazed around his home. I felt his sadness. He looked up at us, his eyes softened in reverent prayer. I shifted uncomfortably.

"We have time," Rowan said kindly.

"That was a courtesy. We waste precious moments." Mica

wrapped the blanket around my shoulders, pulling it up over the wrappings on my head, covering more of me. Rowan mimicked his motions. He looked at us firmly and squeezed my hand reassuringly. "We must be like the quietest wind." His hand in mine, he opened the door and pulled us into the night.

***

It was quiet. Too quiet for a forest full of so many people. I could feel Rowan behind me as Mica drove us on. He kept to narrow alleyways, with dim light filtering out of barred windows and doors. Every hut was closed to the outside. My gut rumbled with the heaviness of its meal and the scent of danger in the dark.

Mica hissed and pulled me down to the ground sharply. Rowan dropped in the same instant. We heard great marching behind us. I saw fear on Mica's face. They had come for us. My heart was racing.

What is the dark one not telling us? Rowan whispered in my thoughts. A great cry rang out and torch lights began to blaze. I could feel movement behind walls, fearful, hiding as the dim lights were blown out and humans cowered in fear. What was this place?

"You. Must. Run." Mica punctuated each word with his teeth. He pointed toward the mountain. "Stay away from the water. Just run!" He pushed me and Rowan took my hand. We were running on broken feet and I wanted to call for Mica to follow. We didn't get more than a few meters when he shouted out in alarm. The hovels around us were thinning. I could taste water on the air. My heart lightened and the blood pounded in my ears so loudly I could not discern that the rushing water was not water, but a moving shadow of smoke and evil. Hands grabbed me roughly from behind and lifted me up into the air as if I weighed no more than driftwood.

"Rowan!" I screamed out loud, the sound startling the breathy silence. A raucous wave of victory went up then and I could see the crowd beneath me, men and women in leathered hides with yellow teeth and mad eyes. They smelled of blood and bone and shit and urine, and I flailed against the hands holding me up until something heavy thudded against my skull.

I was walking through our forest glade, bathed in greens and yellows, covered in sweet daisies and bitter dandelions. I could taste the nectar of the hives that had dwelt in my branches and I was making my way to the nearest village of men, to spend a day among them before taking my turn to slumber. Only I couldn't be. That glade didn't exist anymore. We had woken to its grey and twisted remains. I shook my head and it stabbed me in reply. I remembered every skin I had worn, thick and strong, bending easily with the winds. Surely they had all been truer faces of mine than the one I bore now.

The throbbing in my skull intensified as I was dropped to the ground. I didn't want to open my eyes. I didn't care where we were. I could hear the flickering tongues of torches and it created a bright halo behind my closed eyes. How could I care what befell me when so many had fallen? Why should our fates be any different than those of our own sisters?

"Sister Yew," Rowan spoke out loud. The edge of madness in that command forced my eyes open. We were near the water, in a separate enclosure, on the other side of the wide walls keeping the rest of the city away. Over a hundred men and women stood in a circle, of which my sister and I were at the center. A man with a scarred face leered at me, licking his lips lecherously. Death hid in his breath. He grabbed my hands and tied them to a post beside me. At his touch I tried to crawl backwards, away from him, and the crowd laughed, hands holding me still from behind. Once I was secured, their attention turned.

Rowan was laid out on a table, tied down tightly. Her eyes were on mine. She did not speak. There were no words. The slab beneath her was covered in layers of thick dark crust and I understood how they held City in fear. These people were practiced at this ritual, waiting and hungry. A tall man strode forward, his thick hair strung with bits of broken bone. He alone addressed the crowd.

"What a treat we have tonight. We thought they were all come! And two more birds have filled our nets. Maybe they be the last. Maybe they be the first of more needing the waters only we can provide!" The crowd cheered lowly in agreement as other voices hissed in excited anticipation. The tall man turned to face my sister. "My people are hungry, little birdlies. And nothing sates us longer than the taste of the otherlings." And he went to work. With little ceremony, he raised a long knife high and cut off my sister's leg in one swift stroke.

A scream erupted from my cracked lips as I tried to run, falling when the rope snapped taut. The others around me were silent in reverence, waiting for their share. Rowan's face was twisted in a familiar horror. Her blood dripped sticky onto the ground as the tall man began to cut what he had taken into portions. My sister began to sing a song in a language only the trees know. At the sound of it, several of those in wait crept forward to lick at the blood.

All I could do was watch.

The bit of food in my belly rose and wretched from my mouth, sour in the air. Only her music soothed the quaking in my abdomen. It was a song I hadn't heard her sing since a long forgotten empire of bronze arrows fell overnight. Rowan had sung her sorrow at the death of innocents into that destroyed world and the waters had answered her, rising to claim the earth and the dead. And it had kept rising, pulling the conquerors and their soldiers beneath its depth.

Rowan's eyes were bottomless. Her voice rose in song even as the horde swarmed over her. Enticed by her song, they ripped into her flesh with roughened teeth.

I could not twist away. I would not turn my face. The scar on my thigh twitched and pulled me into a long-remembered state of stillness. As the seconds passed my vision slowed. The blood inside me began to vibrate in harmony to my sister's notes. Her exposed blood was honey-gold. It was glowing.

All around me, the sound of her song became layered with the screams of men. Everywhere her blood touched, great shoots were bursting into life, rooting into flesh and teeth and tongue and earth. The magical saplings fed from the waters in their bodies, and as the men died, a forest sprang into being. The bright stretches of green and yellow quickly climbing up through the skies were blinding against the dark. The roots spreading beneath me began to feed me. I opened my mouth and joined Rowan in song until her voice faded.

The ocean roar of pain and death deafened me as my blood pulsed its own rhythm beneath it. I could feel the magic rising from the new growth, seeking me out. My hands shook in anger and loss, their skin glowing from the inside out. I opened my mouth to start my own song but the hand clamped over my mouth stifled it. Mica put his finger to his lips and cut my bonds free. He kept glancing around at the trees, still growing towards the sky, white birches and dark rowans. I spied an oak creeping towards the shore, a willow breaking through a rooftop. I knew there were more scattered among the birch, ash, hawthorn, juniper, hazel, and yew. An impossible grove. I was immobilized between grief and love.

"We have to leave," my new friend said, cutting the ropes that tied me. He dragged me backwards, whispering in my ear. "What few cannibals are left will want you dead. It won't be long before the rest of City comes for you as well." I heard his words as I stared in wonder around me. *My beautiful sister...* For me, the sounds of dying men faded beneath their canopy, spreading out above my head, groaning with unbearable growing pains. Mica was struggling with me and we fell into thickening roots. His voice was quick in my ear. "They will be talking about whether to bleed you for wood to burn or wood to build."

"These trees are alive!" The pull of the roots beneath my body was too much. I could just stay here. I could stay and take a more familiar skin. I could stop walking. The children would protect me, I was sure of it. And I could protect them. It was our purpose. Hope fluttered behind my breastbone.

"Sister." Mica's voice was strained. I took my hand from the flesh of the smooth root I fell on and turned to look at him. There was a cut above his eye and his arms bore welts and bruises. He had fought them for us. His eyes were sharp. "City has need. They will burn it all."

I shook my head and kept shaking it. The forest was a miracle, a gift given for a life taken. I could not bear more death.

"We must get far from here," Mica groaned. "You understand me fine?" He wrapped his arms around my waist and hauled me up out of the earth. My chest was made of stone as he pulled me away from the sounds of death. He was shaking but I felt nothing. My ribs did not vibrate or care about the shrill shrieking of sapling roots wrapping around bone, breaking them into shards in their genesis. I wanted to break my own bones and free myself from this human skin. I did not want to wear their face. The death of my world had trapped me in theirs. "Can you walk?" Mica yelled in my ear.

"If I had wings I would fly." I was aware of his hands guiding me through the cannibal homes of wood and metal until we didn't see any more buildings. Just stone and grass and waterline. No one guarded the shore. Certainly they had been drawn to the destruction in the camp. Even those who had lived in fear of the cannibals would be moths drawn to the flaming wreckage of what had become of them. Of what my sister had become.

"Shh," Mica said gently to me. I looked up at him and realized I was crying. "You are safe with me."

"So I am yours?" I asked bitterly, aware of the human emotion creeping through me. "I am not yours to salvage, cyote!" I shuddered, digging my fingers into his arms until he winced in pain. I could feel life, threatening to spill over, biting at the edges of my fingertips. I could feel my limbs longing to stretch and grow and rip through his bones, through all of their bones for what they had done-

Mica bit back a choked cry and I released him, retracting my nails from his skin. He was bleeding and I was shaking. The water lapped at the shore behind us in small waves like prayers. The new water spoke in petitions rather than demands. It was asking of me and I could feel the call and response of a new song running in my veins, for we also spoke the language of water and wind. I could feel the anger ebbing. I shrugged what was human off. Mica rubbed his arms, blinking back moisture, petitioning me for forgiveness.

"You don't belong to us. None of your world belongs to us. You are the last hope we have. I would do anything to keep you safe."

"I do not want to be kept." I turned to follow the shore

towards the mountain and we stumbled in silence through the
longest dark of the night.

***

We walked without words until the city behind us was a
speck of garbage on the horizon and grey had lightened the sky.
We rested against a clump of rocks near the base of the
mountainous rise. From up here, I could see all the edges of the
water and it caught my breath. Mica raised his eyebrow at me. "I
remember when all the eye could see was water. It was hard to
believe it was not an ocean."

"An ocean?" It was not a word he knew.

"You could travel for days on the water and not see land.
Weeks even."

"I do not believe that could be possible."

I stared at the darker shape looming above us. "But this
mountain was not a mountain. I remember. There was more than
enough water for everyone."

Mica leaned against a rock and I saw the cut on his head
was still flowing slow blood. I removed the wrapping that held
my hair up and ripped a length from it. I did not need to look at
him to know he was staring at me in awe as I wrapped his wound,
my hands bright against his dark skin. Our hair always gave us
away. I touched his shoulders and all of my secret days spent
dancing among the humans flashed through my thoughts. Mica
lifted a hand and timidly touched one of the pale-green hair
fronds hanging over my chest, almost translucent in my
heightened state.

I touched the scar on the other side of his face and I knew
that I had the power to heal it for him. But I wouldn't. My new
friend leveled his gaze at me, my hands on his shoulders, his
hand on my hair. His eyes were like flint, with flecks of
huckleberry. I watched his wonder turn to stone.

"I know what you mean to do." His eyes were
unforgiving. "You cannot! There is much we don't know. You
were there." Why should I care when the freshest sounds in my
heart were those of teeth ripping flesh and wood groaning in

sudden flight? What could I say that he would understand?

"My Sisters and I spent centuries breathing in seasons, taking turns witnessing the passages of men. Sister Oak sang me songs of all she witnessed while I slept. And yet, we're not sure when the end came. We woke to fire and smoke and we were dying in our wooden skins. My sister chose the worst death imaginable for one of my kind, rather than share the song of the undoing that occurred. I have no answers for you."

I remembered when humans were an occasional curiosity to birch eyes. I remembered when the land was peopled with trees instead of humans. This earth was preparing to sleep again. But the birth of Rowan's forest had woken something in the water, and I carried it inside me. What to do with it? To stay in this human form would mean to die a human death. To change my skin would mean to die at the hands of men. Living in this world would not be possible, but perhaps, the next world…

Mica could see the change in my eyes. He opened his mouth and closed it again with a groaning sigh. The dullness in his eyes sparked a fire in me. "The chance for men to change their fate has long passed. You must give us a chance."

"I will protect you," he promised.

"You may have to," I answered, twisting my hair back under its wrapping. I could feel the rippling of the magic settling in my blood. Mica settled his bag securely across his shoulder and continued up the rocks. I followed. I would walk until I could walk no more. Then my waters would feed the earth, far from the eyes of man. We would be remembered in the groves of birch and yew, of rowan, hazel and juniper, of oak, ash, and thorn. And something of my world would survive.

Monster Godmother

Lyn Thorne-Alder

"Medic!"

"Coming, coming." The scream had come from the north. Winnie dodged a flying rock and two fireballs to get around the blockade, then dropped to her belly to slink the last ten feet. The enemy was still laying down machine-gun fire — were they creating their bullets out of thin air?

…They could be…

The earthworks gave Winnie just enough cover. She could hear the bullets overhead but as long as she didn't put too much hump in her worming she was going to get the patient just fine.

"Me-*dic*!" She was almost there; the shout blasted her eardrums.

"Coming, coming!" Gunfire followed her movement. If they used a rocket…

Winnie hadn't meant to get involved in this war. She had been living in this land for a long time but she had no interest in dying on it – or for it. Let the enemy come. She had planned on waiting out the fight in a nice cabin on a nice mountainside, maybe somewhere with a view. Here she was instead, belly down in the dirt, hoping nobody shot her rear end off.

Nobody wasted a rocket on her flat butt. She made it to the end of the earthworks, to the ad-hoc foxhole where someone was biting back screams into something closer to whimpers.

"Med— oh. There you are. He's gut-shot."

"Got it, got it." She'd actually been *in* that cabin. It was a very nice cabin. And now she was elbow-deep in somebody else's guts. "Gun or grenade or something worse?"

"Gun. Machine gun." The friend was the one who had been shouting. From the looks of things, the guy with the belly ripped open hadn't been conscious since he'd gotten hit. And the friend was looking out, not looking into the bunker, even as he answered questions. "Can you..." Now, he turned to look at Winnie. "Are you...?"

"Yes. And yes. But only if I work fast and I'm not interrupted. Can you cover me?"

"Got it. They're mostly focusing on our left flank anyway. Something over there they want. I mean, I'm guessing. These people don't make any sense."

"What's your name..." She checked rank even as she pulled out her kit and laid it on the cleanest place she could find. "...Private?"

"Smith, ma'am, Tanner Smith."

"Good man, Smith. Now if I am going to put your friend Private Colburn here back together..."

"Right, right. Sorry, ma'am." He shifted, rifle ready, to cover her.

Good enough. She pushed her consciousness into the wound. Bullets had perforated Colburn's intestines and made hash of his abdominal muscles, but the damage had happened just minutes before she got there and his body had barely begun poisoning itself. She could fix this. She could fix this if she had a few minutes.

She probably only had a few seconds. They might be focusing on the other front right now, but that wouldn't stop them from moving over here when they realized their target wasn't where they were looking.

Seconds, right. Seal the holes, eject the bullet. She murmured the Words of her magic under her breath — Smith might have figured it out, but that was no reason to rub his nose in it — and pulled the man's guts back together.

He opened his eyes as she was suturing his stomach closed. "Monster!"

"Yes, admitted." She didn't look up from her work. "Now would you please hold still and let the monster keep saving your life?"

The magic she used for healing took too much energy for her to maintain a glamour. The young man was staring at the horns curling into her hair and the way her ears pointed upwards like a cat's. As Changes went, it wasn't that extreme — but it clearly marked her as inhuman.

"Monster," he repeated.

"I've heard worse."

"Monsters!"

"Damn, damn." Smith dove over them. *"Down! Grenade!"*

Winnie flattened herself over her patient as the world went white.

***

Winnie hadn't meant to get involved in the war.

When the creatures that called themselves gods had invaded Earth, they hadn't expected resistance. From the looks of them, from the way they spoke and the way the carried themselves, they hadn't expected anything but worship.

They had been driven off the planet, back to Ellehem, over a millennium ago, and they clearly thought that nothing had changed on earth in all that time. They clearly assumed that none like them had stayed, or thought that if any 'gods-children' of their ilk who remained would be weak, not worth their concern.

Within six months of the gates reopening, within half a year of the invasion from Ellehem, both humans and Earth-bound gods-children had proven the returned gods very wrong indeed.

Another half year later, the wars raged on. Gods and gods-children fought epic battles, destroying cities in their wake. Humans sent armies against both of them, fighting those who were not-quite-human indiscriminately.

People were going to die, but people always died. Winnie had done her best to stay out of it as long as she could. Cities fell. Countries fell. All around her humans, gods, and gods-children died. Those returned from Ellehem had not expected resistance, but they got it in spades.

***

"I swear, this is going to be the death of us."

Winnie woke in a tent and in pain. She blinked until the dim light no longer assaulted her eyes, checked her body to be certain it was all still there — it had to be; there wasn't a part of it that didn't hurt — and then checked her surroundings for threats.

She was fairly certain that neither Privates Smith nor Colburn were actually threats to her. If they'd wanted to end her, they probably would have shoved a stake in her heart, stuffed garlic down her throat, and cut her head off.

Not that it would have *worked*. But then, at least, she'd have known they wanted her dead.

"It's going to be the death of *us* at least." Private Colburn looked a lot better than his buddy did. He also looked a lot better than the last time Winnie had met him. And he looked about two hundred percent better than Winnie felt at the moment. "Hey, the medic is awake."

"Haven't you seen the casualties? Haven't you heard what happened to L.A.? I mean, forget about NYC, there's a *crater* in L.A." Smith pulled himself into a sitting position. "Hey, Medic. How're you feeling?"

"Like death." Winnie thought about sitting up and decided against it. "What hit us?"

"Some sort of frag grenade. Doctor says it was full of wood fragments. They're still trying to get them all out of you and Smith. But hey, you're the miracle worker, aren't you? Can't you just wiggle your nose and fix everything?"

Wood. Winnie felt her hands go cold. "Did he say what sort of wood?"

"He said, and I quote, 'I'm a doctor, not a botanist, Jim.' Man's a bit of a nerd. But then he said that you were healing like a human — that is, not. And, no offense, Monster Medic, but you're not human."

"None taken. I'd noticed." She tapped one of her horns weakly, and then decided that was a bad idea. Even her *horns* hurt.

"Wood." She looked between the two of them. "What

were you saying?"

"Oh." Color rose to Smith's cheeks. "Just that this war was going to kill us all."

"I've lived through quite a few of them so far, and not one of them has been fatal."

"Did you just..." Colburn, it turned out, was a giggler. Winnie grinned, then found that smiling hurt, too.

"Well, I had to do something. So where are we? This isn't the med tent."

"It's a Mobile Army Surgical Hospital unit." Smith couldn't quite hold back the chuckle. "We're seriously in M.A.S.H."

"Damn, it's been decades since I've been in one of those." Winnie tried stretching. Stretching she could handle. "So way back. I should get back out there."

"We should all get back out there." Colburn leaned forward. "You've lived through wars?"

"Still here." She thumped her chest inadvisably. "Ow. In pain, but still here."

"What's it like?"

***

She hadn't meant to be in that war, either. She'd been more or less minding her own business, hunting furs and very, very surreptitiously serving as a village physick and midwife, perfectly happy ignoring the fact that she was a colonist under the purview of England – She thought it was England. Somewhere along the way she'd lost track.

Then the war had started up around her and it had become very clear that while she might not be taking sides, the war did not care at all about that. She was either going to be for someone or against them.

With bound breasts and a man's jacket, Winnie slipped into the war and found the medic's tent.

It wasn't her first war. Wars tended to move through the land of the quiet and the out-of-the-way, and often the only choices given were fight or die. In her last war, she'd been drafted. In this one, she found what served as doctors in that day in age and attached her teenaged-boy persona to them.

"Help," they screamed. Or "God help me," when there was nothing but Winnie. She did what she could for them – as much magic as wouldn't be noticed, as much medicine as the day and time knew – and moved onto the next before they died of blood loss.

***

"Bloody." Winnie found she'd closed her eyes; she opened them to look at Colburn. "Bloody, messy, and full of screaming."

"Sounds like here." Smith tried to laugh, but it caught in his throat. "I mean... they just brought in a guy missing half his leg and both of his hands."

"Yeah." Winnie swallowed. "I've found that some things really don't change. One of those is the blood. The doctors can save more, now—"

"What about your miracles?"

"Well, Private Colburn, miracles work just fine, when one, you're not full of hawthorn, two, no one's shouting *monster* at you, and three, someone isn't trying to light you on fire for *being* a monster."

He had the grace to look at least a little embarrassed. "We're fighting the monsters. I mean, we're fighting these, what, 'gods?' Things that came back from somewhere? And they have things like horns and wings and hooves and purple skin... and then I wake up and there's a girl with elf ears and horns leaning over me."

"Some of them left and returned. Some never left." Winne shrugged.

"Right, I got that. 'Returned gods' and all. Just surprised me."

"Wait, hawthorn?" Smith leaned over. His left leg was chewed up, like the world's biggest dog had been gnawing on it. "What's that have to do with anything?"

Winnie concentrated, pushing her will through the pain

and the haze of poison, and forced a piece of the wood out of her arm. It welled up through the skin like a shark cresting out of the water, and she yanked it out before it could get away. "It's poison to us. It stops our magic — us and the gods, we're the same biologically." It was the shortest, most oversimplified explanation she could give, but she could see from the look on the Privates' faces that she'd gotten her point across. "Deadly in large doses."

"And someone tossed a frag grenade of that shit into our foxhole." Smith shook his head. "They were aiming at you."

"Which means…"

"Which means our medic is going to lay down and let me finish pulling wood out of her, while you two boys leave her alone." The doctor, who looked more Hawkeye than Bones, muscled his way in between Smith and Winnie. "I saw what you did there, miss. You saved young Colburn's life."

"Just doing my job…" She was saved from coming up with anything else to say by the wail of a siren. "Shit, that's the attack alarm, isn't it?"

"Gear up, girl. We'll evacuate through the—"

The back of the building smashed in, collapsing what Winnie sincerely hoped was the supplies section.

"—back door."

Winne swallowed. "I have an idea."

* * *

They'd gone out the back because the enemy was in the front. Winnie had been leading, the last time she'd ever taken a leadership position. She'd picked the route — into the mountains, more specifically towards a mountain that the enemy was deeply superstitious about.

The plan wasn't to escape so much as it was to survive the night. Their side was vastly outnumbered and reinforcements would not be able to make it until the morning. If then. The if then was the stuff Winnie's nightmares were made of. What if the ships never arrived?

They had to make it out, one way or the other, so they

took the old passageways into the mountain. Legends — their legends, the enemy's legends; if you went back long enough they were the same stories — said that the passages had been carved by an angry god. Looking at the tunnels — sleek like glass, smooth and perfectly circular tubes — Winnie could believe it. Still, nothing said the god — or whatever it was; Winnie did not believe in gods — was still there. And she had a team to get out the other side.

Only seven of them survived the earthquake. In the night, she still woke hearing the god-thing's laughter.

Seven out of seventy. She'd stood up on a broken leg and walked them out of there anyway.

***

"It's not a good plan." Winnie looked around the room — at Smith and Colburn, at the doctor, at ten others: injured soldiers, nurses, an aide. "It's not a good plan at all. The plus is that if we take it, we have a chance of getting out of here. If we don't…"

"If we don't," the doctor who was not a botanist cut in, "Then we have to do a heroic last stand, and let me tell you, I got into medicine to do anything but heroic last stands, at least not the sort that involve weapons pointed at me."

"Exactly. It's not a good plan, just the best one we've got. I know this land." Winnie gestured through the tent wall. "I know this land very well. I have been living here for… a while."

"Do you mean a couple years?" The doctor tilted his head.

"I mean a couple centuries." Winnie paused, watching each of them. "I know that there has been nothing but distrust for my kind since the war began. But some of us never left. And some of us were born here." Watching their faces, she decided a little more explanation might be in order. "Millennia ago, the creatures called gods fought. Most of them were dragged back to Ellehem, the gates sealed behind them. Some stayed here, to guard, to live in secret. Generations passed; empires passed. People had children. Those children had children." She gestured at herself.

"And now I have a plan. There is a cave system…" She winced, but this one hadn't been built by a gods-child, or if it had, it had been long before she came to this country. "And if this tent is where I think it is, the entrance is a quick run — hobble, in some cases — that way." She pointed again, knowing she was pointing through the enemy. "Or, if we're clever about it, ten feet down."

"Why should we trust you?"

Someone always asked that. She met the gaze of the injured Lieutenant who asked it this time. "You shouldn't. I'm a medic – I don't lead. But I want to survive this war as much as you do, and right now, the easiest way to do that is ten feet down. And, if the good doctor will help me pull the last of the hawthorn out of me, I can get us there."

"I thought you were a medic." The woman in the back had been quiet enough that Winnie had assumed she was unconscious. Now she sat up, revealing a broken arm. "Now you're going to tell us you're good at earthworks, too?"

Winnie felt herself smiling in a way that had nothing to do with humor. "I have had a while to branch out. And I had cause to learn how to move giant piles of rock."

Private Colburn spoke up. "Ma'am – you said war hasn't killed you yet. *How many wars?*"

Winnie pursed her lips. "Many. I don't always get involved, but often the war chooses to involve me. Three on this continent, maybe four, before I ended up here."

"Then I think… sorry, sirs." He nodded to the doctor and the Lieutenant. "The medic saved my life. I'm pretty sure she's on our side. And I'm pretty sure she knows what she's doing."

***

She had no idea what she was doing; she had barely any more of an idea why she was here.

She had a plan, of sorts, but it was more of a goal — get the children away from the immediate threat, and get them to a place where they could be safe for a while.

And she had a target location, slightly more concrete than her goal — the hills to the north, where farmers did not like intruders and the war had not yet touched.

More importantly than either of those, she had seventeen children who were relying on her. Their parents were all dead, dying, or fled; their families were missing or had cast them out. She, a monster hiding in human skin, was the only thing they had.

And monsters who had more claim on humanity than she — and more claim on monstrousness — were coming for them.

They were young, most of them. Young enough to overlook a little magic? She hoped so, strongly, while she murmured the magic under her breath, bending the trees together for shelter, opening a tunnel in the earth for travel.

"Are you a fairy?" One small child, ragged and dirty, dared to ask what might have been on all their minds.

She considered her answer for a moment, but there was little time to spend on thoughts right now. "Yes. I am the fairy godmother to all of you."

***

"And there. That's the last of it, as far as I can tell. This stuff really stops you from…" The doctor – his name really was Benjamin, but it wasn't Pierce, it was Perry – waved his free hand.

"It also kills us." Winnie thought it was important to point that out. "But yes, hawthorn in our bloodstream will first stop us from doing magic. Also, it burns like hell."

"Interesting." Dr. Perry nodded again. "So, you're good now?"

The crash of another missile landed near them. "Yes. Where did they get missiles… never mind. I'm sure a god can come up with a rocket or two. Okay, everyone stand back as close to the edge of the tent as you can get. Mobile people, please help the non-mobiles. We've got to get this done fast, and we've got to…" Something crashed over the already-smashed back of the tent. Winnie shut up and got to work.

The earth here was dry and hard. It hadn't been worked in

years. This part of the county had been so deep in a depression that farming had dried up, along with almost every other industry. It was not the ideal land for creating a hole in the ground, but it was what she had to work with.

Winnie sent her consciousness into the hole, as she would with a wound, as she had all those years — decades — centuries ago when she made an escape passage for the children. Those children were so long gone, now, but their smiles stayed with her. *I will be your fairy godmother.*

The ground shifted, rose, and subsided. Winnie ignored the movement, ignored the alarmed shouts, ignored the bombs landing nearby. This had to be done carefully. A ten-foot fall wasn't that bad — but it wasn't a picnic, either. "Rope." She spat the word out between her magic. "Anyone?"

"Got it." Something crashed, far too close to the tent. Winnie closed her eyes and kept working. It wasn't *coming*, it wasn't working. Too much hawthorn in the blood, too much blood lost. Even the daughters of gods had their limitations.

"Blast it…" She opened her eyes. The hole was only an indentation. Gunfire rattled closer and closer. "I can't…"

"Here." Private Colburn grabbed an IV stand and began beating at the earth. "We've got this, Monster Ma'am. Down here, you said? Right here? Come *on*, Smith."

"I'm on one leg, if you hadn't noticed."

"Then sit and dig, I don't care."

Winnie took a breath. Maybe it would help. She closed her eyes and summoned every bit of energy she could find.

Almost there, almost… Someone took her hand. She squeezed it and kept murmuring the words, over and over again. She could feel the earth shifting, not only under her magic but under the privates' pounding as well. Almost there. Almost. "Stand back." The dirt shifted and finally gave way. "Got it."

There was not enough rope to be found – only about twelve feet – but they made do, sliding down the side of the hole on army cots, the able—legged supporting those who couldn't hold weight. Winnie held it together until the last of them had slid into the cave below, then dropped herself down after them. She lost consciousness as she hit the rocks below.

***

"You said you were my fairy godmother."

The woman was old, now. It had been fifty years or more since Winnie had led the children through the underground caves to safety, and, while the years had passed quickly for Winnie, they had not for the woman lying in the bed.

"I did." Winnie nodded. "And I have looked after you and yours all these years."

"I didn't believe you, you know. Fairy godmothers happen in stories." The woman was old, now, her hair white. Winnie closed her eyes to remember the girl with the dark hair and the wide eyes.

"I know." She smiled, although she did not open her eyes yet. "I remember. But now?"

The girl's hand stroked Winnie's hair — still black, still long. "It's been a lifetime."

It had been a moment. "I know. And I persist."

"You'll be here forever, won't you?"

"At least for a very long time. Or until something kills me."

"I remember the farmer with the pitchfork."

Winnie did, too. Monster he'd called her, while she had been too weak to hold up her glamour. "That does happen on occasion."

"And still you saved us."

Winnie hadn't meant to get involved — never meant to get involved. "You needed saving."

***

Winnie woke to the uncomfortable sensation of being dragged on some sort of litter. When had this sort of thing become a habit?

Opening her eyes revealed very little: the light was dim, the air was cold, and they were moving. "I can walk." Her voice was a croak, which startled her. What had she... ah. The hole. "I can make light."

Her litter stopped bumping along. "Good." She thought Private Colburn sounded amused rather than relieved, or maybe she just hoped that. "Doctor Bones says there's a fork in the way up ahead, and it's pitch black in both directions."

"We're already to the fork?" She closed her eyes again, bringing forth the memory of the cave system. She'd fallen into it by accident, back when she'd first come to this land. It had taken her days to find her way out — not the most pleasant of memories. "I hate caves."

"You're the one that brought us down here, Ma'am monster."

"Well, I hate bombs more. I hope they don't use bunker busters."

"Don't see why they would. We don't have any bunkers." He offered her a hand and, glad nobody could see her flush in this light, Winnie took it. "Do you think anyone's left alive back up there?"

"I think we're alive. And right now, I am going to focus on how much that matters to me. All right?"

"Yes, ma'am."

Her ankle was turned, but not too badly. She limped to the front of the line, pulling up the energy for a small light spell as she went. She was lucky that didn't take much — her tank was still hovering very near empty.

"We want to take the left here, and then the next right, and then lefts thereon. We're going to end up aboveground in the middle of a cow pasture..." Winnie sighed. "It was a cow pasture. I don't know what it is anymore, but it's a long way away from the battle and that's what matters."

"Thank you, soldier."

They limped along, moving none too fast. The sounds of battle were almost completely muffled, down here, but on occasion the ground would shake, or the roof of the cave system would drop some pebbles on them.

"How many people do you think are alive up there?" Private Colburn had attached himself to her side, perhaps worried because she kept swaying. The light spell really wasn't *that* hard, not all things considered.

"In the world?" Winnie pursed her lips. "Depends on how bad it is. The last I heard before the army plowed through here, the major players were as badly hit as we were. And what was the last news count?"

"Monsters watch the news?"

"How else will we know when the monster balls are?" She smiled sidelong at him and hoped he recognized a joke when he heard it. But his question was no joke at all. She gave it due consideration.

"There's probably at least a quarter of the population left. I mean, there's going to be the supply problem — a lot of these battles have been fought over farmland... you didn't want that much of an answer, did you?"

"How can you be so casual about it?"

"Casual?" Winnie sighed. "No. I am not casual. It's just that I've seen war before. The first time, I thought it was the end of the world. This time—"

"They blew up L.A. They destroyed New York. It is the end of the world."

What was left of the world had a sense of the dramatic because at that moment they rounded a bend into the sunlight. It was weak sunlight, filtered through weeds and end-of-day thin, but it was sunlight.

"It's just a stumbling block."

***

Winnie hadn't wanted to get involved in the war. Let the so-called returned gods fight the would-be heroes that had stayed. Let the humans do what they would, fight or bow in worship or run away. She had been knee-deep in gore and death for far too much of her long life. People, after all, died – no matter what you did.

She'd ensconced herself in a tidy cabin up on the mountainside. It was a nice place — very few modern conveniences, but then again, she had lived far longer without those than with. It had a very nice view of the countryside.

The view ended up being her biggest problem. From her

*front porch, she could see the war encroaching. She could see the
returned god who had taken over the nearby city; she could see
the army he'd bewitched.*

*She had once told a child that she was their fairy
godmother.*

*She had once told a dying woman that she saved people
because they needed saving. People died.*

*Winnie had stared at the growing war and wondered what
happened if humanity died.*

***

The view from the cabin wasn't the most beautiful
anymore; Winnie had coaxed some trees into growing up quickly,
both to hide their shelter from view and to hide the carnage
below. She sat on the railing, looking in at the people she'd
saved.

Private Colburn — Brandon — hopped up next to her. He
didn't really look at her; he almost never did when she had her
Glamour covering her horns. He stared at the cabin, instead. "I
caught a radio dispatch."

"Mm?" They could still get those some days. It was more
and more rare, however. They weren't in the best location for
such things — and there weren't many people left bothering.

"They've been counting. Looking for gods, looking for
monsters, but mostly just counting what's left."

There weren't many, she had a feeling. They'd been out
here a month and found less than ten other survivors. "How
bad?"

"They figure it's about ninety percent gone." Now, he
looked at her. She could see the way his throat worked, like he
was trying to swallow more information than he could handle.
"Nine out of ten people gone. What do you *do* with that?"

He trusted her to know. How to tell him that she'd never
seen a war this bad, that she'd never seen the end this near?

But she had.

"You do what we did in the cave." What she had in that
cave so many centuries ago, when some gods-child or monster

brought it down on her. "You pick up what you've got left, and you keep going."

"Just like that?"

"Well… maybe you cry once in a while. I know I do. But then you keep going."

"Why? What's the point? There's nothing left!"

"There's you. There's me." She patted his leg. "There's thirty million people. The daylight is out there, kid, and somewhere, someone is counting on you to get them out of the cave. You've just got to keep walking."

Small Victories

E.V. O'Day

Aer bent to her knees before the rusty pond and flared her nostrils wide over the surface. The rusty discolouration caused by the sediments below didn't make her pause. The total lack of plant life in and around the water made her think twice. But she was thirsty. Tongue-like-sandpaper and saliva-like-glue kind of thirsty. She sniffed again, tasting the pungent sulphur stuck to the back of her throat, intensified by every inhale in this wasteland.

The water seemed alright.

Unable to quell the insistence of her dehydrated body any longer, she dipped her fingertips through the pliant surface. Within the seconds it took for the sides of her hands to meet to form a cup, the pain set in. Aer kicked away from the pond's edge, splashing the substance across her front as she thrashed.

"Told you so," Kara said as she grabbed a handful of dirt and smeared the sandy mess across Aer's chest to absorb the wetness.

"Shut up, just shut up," Aer whined as she rubbed her hands in the grey earth to remove any trace of the acid.

Kara sighed long and loud before she stepped away, wiping her dirty hands on her dry, cracked leathers.

Aer pulled her hands free of the dead ground and inspected the damage. The flesh knit back together as she watched, covering the bone visible at her fingertips and knuckles. Were she not a valkyrie her stunt would have meant her death. Survival for non-immortal warrioresses was currently at an all-time low, even when you had fully functional hands. She sighed over the state of her cracked, ragged nails surrounded by new pink skin. Manicures had gone the way of civilization and

Aer was still depressed about it.

Standing, she smoothed back the strands of hair that had come dislodged from her braid and couldn't decide which fate she would have preferred: life, or death. Goddess knew life sucked the big one right now.

Aer turned her back on the misleading pond and took in the barren landscape around her and Kara. From the direction they came a blizzard drove snow –not the nice powder that cascaded softly from the sky that she loved to ski on, but the stuff that rained down like razors– in icy cyclones. Yet yards away, the storm stopped like it smacked up against an invisible barrier where the desert-scape began. At least there were no signs of flash flooding. Their travels had been extended too long thanks to currents that preferred to sweep them in the wrong direction.

What happens when you mix nostalgic, ambrosia-filled Greek, Norse, and Hindu trouble-makers with egos bigger than their brains together? Not a damn good thing, Aer fumed. Again.

The sun glared off of spiky rocks and ash ridden terrain, making Aer sweat in her armour. She might as well have been on Mars for all the life she saw: no trees or grasses, no insects or game, no water save the puddle of poison at her back. The surface had been subjected to a heat hotter than humans could create. *Nothing* barely remained, and the nothing that had survived the god-sent fire was toxic to whatever clung to life.

Not that that, or Kara's nagging, could stop Aer from trying to disprove that fact. The "water" had called to her like a misleading siren and she'd listened. She hated sirens. With any luck the bitches were all dead.

"Nice shirt," Kara said. Aer looked down to see caked dirt and an imperfect gaping O where leather and steel once rested over her heart. A few half-rings remained along the edges where the acid stopped dissolving them thanks to Kara's quick thinking.

"Dammit! I've had this mail since the dark ages."

"Your intention was not to reveal your navel with that stunt?"

"Shut up," Aer said, stomping away.

Kara caught up with her. "I might have a dollar bill tucked into my boot if you give me a moment."

"Shut. Up." Aer repeated.

She led them towards the base of the long-dead volcano directly in their path. Antofalla's conical shape spread more horizontal than vertical but the mountain still provided one hell of a hill for them to climb. The bit of plant life on its middle promised water and the altitude promised gentle coolness. Two things Aer desperately needed to re-experience.

She wiped sweat from her brow as thoughts of the idiotic instigators of the end popped into her mind, swiftly followed by a strange ache just below where her top now opened. If she were human she would have asked a doctor to take a look at her persistently aching sternum. And if any hospitals remained.

Along with the medical centres, everything that had made her long immortal life seem less tedious was gone. A few pockets of less affected places where humans could still survive existed, but emphasize few and toss in a far between. Places where people weren't fighting over resources were rarer.

Aer unclenched her jaw as she thought back on the plagues she witnessed ravage humanity over the ages –bubonic, smallpox, malaria. People always bounced back. Hell, she'd seen humans come back from having nuclear weapons dropped on them. But life as they and the immortals who had lived in their shadows knew it was very gone.

Aer was certain the earth wasn't coming back from this. Which left her, Kara, and all of the earth-bound valkyries a job to do before returning to the god-plane. To wait out eternity with no adventures to hunt down. The pain in her chest intensified; when she tried to take a deep breathe to dispel it, her diaphragm seized and she gasped.

Inside Antofalla, the fury queen, Megaera, was preparing to host a summit open to all immortals. Aer hoped she intended to lead a fight.

"Do you see something?" Kara asked, stopping to draw the sword dangling on her left hip halfway out of its scabbard. She scanned the terrain they faced.

"The past," Aer said.

"Ah," Kara re-sheathed her sword. "Do not worry, we will get to the summit soon and plan the beheadings of those three nitwits and the dipshit."

"What if they don't want to kill them?" Aer voiced for the hundredth time.

"You and I and our sisters will do it anyway," Kara said. "I cannot see the furies and harpies not wanting blood for this, but if they do not, more for us."

Aer smiled. All valkyries were birthed by the same goddess, Freya, who bedded the greatest warriors permitted into Valhalla to father her powerful daughters. Valkyries carried the immortal power of their mother and the temperaments of their fathers. To say the women were normally battle-thirsty would be an understatement. To say they weren't foaming at the mouth for the chance to spill blood now would be stupid.

"I want their heads on pikes," Aer said.

"We will pop out their eyes and make jack-o-lanterns out of their skulls, too." They laughed at the image.

"All in good time, right?"

"Indeed. Do you see that copse of tall brush there?" Kara pointed to a spot halfway up the mountain.

"What about it?" Aer squinted at the spot.

"Race you!" Kara tripped Aer before running as fast as she could.

***

"Blessed Freya, I feel like a mountain goat." Kara laughed as she ran into the clearing, falling onto the biggest rock there. Aer wasn't far behind and sat across from her, landing in a clanking heap.

"Yeah, a cheating mountain goat." Aer imitated a ram's call and they burst into giggles.

The mountain-side rang with silence after their laugher subsided, emphasizing the crack of a twig as it snapped nearby. Aer stopped smiling and sat up like a steel spike had replaced her spine. In silent agreement, both women stood back to back with swords drawn and scanned the tall bushes surrounding them. After whining about the lack of life for so long, Aer found herself cursing now that there was cover for enemies to hide in.

"Who goes there," Aer called into the woods. She and Kara held their breaths as they waited for more noise.

"I am not an enemy," a male voice declared from Aer's left. She shifted her stance so that she faced that direction head-on. She felt Kara shift behind her.

"Can you see him?" Kara whispered.

"Show yourself," Aer called.

A broad man made his way out of the sparse scrub in front of Aer, grumbling as a thorny branch nearly six feet off the ground slapped him in the face. With his arms raised over his head he was unprotected from nature. "I wasn't spying. I heard voices and came to investigate. I'm alone."

Aer hushed him with a gesture and indicated that he should get to his knees. She and Kara listened to the silence for moments longer. Kara tapped her shoulder so Aer approached the man widely while her sister headed off into the trees to make sure no one else hid around them.

Positioned behind the man, Aer kicked his back to get him face down in the rocky soil. He grunted when she jumped knees first on top of him and tied his wrists together with a length of rope she carried for such occasions. "Your name," she demanded, as she tied his ankles to his hands.

"Thrake," he said.

"A naiad?"

"Yes," Thrake confirmed. "You are?"

"Aer the Merciful." She sniffed the air before she stood off him and glanced around the campsite. He smelled overly musky, with an undertone she couldn't place. She inhaled deeply and sneezed.

"I didn't know there was such a thing as a merciful valkyrie."

"There isn't," Aer informed him, tears burning her eyes as she fought a second sneeze.

"Too bad. Here I was hoping the three of us could have a good time."

"Only in your dreams, naiad. And if my sister hears you even thinking about dreaming of her, I can assure you she'll gut you like a deer. With her rusty blade."

"What kind of valkyrie carries rusty weapons?"

"Kara the Wild."

"This is where I say eep, isn't it?" Thrake asked as he put his forehead to the ground.

"Only if our reputations precede us," Aer pointed out.

"Eep."

Kara returned just as the naiad started softly banging his forehead against the ground. "Did you find anything?"

"His tracks and his alone," Kara said. "There was an odd trampled patch that smelled funny, though."

The naiad shrugged as well as he could. "When nature calls…"

"Ew," Kara cringed as her eyes roved over the man whose jeans, t-shirt, and pale skin were smeared with dirt. Then she grinned at her sister. "You hog tied him?"

"He's a naiad," Aer said as though that explained it. Kara nodded while the male raised his head as much as he was able in his position. Aer explained for his benefit, "All male nymphs are pigs. Duh."

"Hey!"

"Did he tell you his name?" Kara asked, ignoring the outraged sputtering at her back as she returned to her rock.

"Thrake." Aer followed her sister.

"I resent you calling me a pig!" The water nymph yelled.

"Not a name that I recognize. He must be of a younger generation." Kara said. "What do you want to do with him?"

"The reputations of my kind have been blown out of proportion."

"Do you think we should take him to the summit?" Aer asked.

"I'm not hauling him up the rest of this volcano," Kara said, removing a gleaming knife from her belt and cleaning under her nails with the tip.

"Just because a few water nymphs were known to let loose the rest of us are thrown into the skank category, how is that fair?"

"I'm not hauling him up the mountain, either," Aer replied, letting her lank hair down so that she could re-braid it.

What she wouldn't give for a nice hot shower with her favourite body wash.

"Warrior maidens are known to kill first and ask questions later, but do I go around calling you homicidal maniacs? No."

"I say we make him climb at sword point," Aer said. "At least it'll shut him up."

"What about your mother and fathers, huh? Great origins there. Do I hold it against you? No."

"Speaking of which." Kara removed a strip of cloth from the top of her leather boot and walked over to the man.

"Just because naiads are superior flirts we're constantly thrown under the bus like—what are you doing?"

Kara grabbed a fist full of the naiad's hair. "Wait!" She tugged his head up as far as his neck would allow, then stuffed the material into his flapping mouth, far enough that he couldn't spit it out.

Aer laughed at the face the naiad made before Kara released him. The cloth had been in her sister's boot for weeks and she couldn't imagine what it must taste like.

"It is your turn to take watch," Kara informed her as she skipped back.

"Is not, I stayed up late last night."

"Did not. You are such a liar."

"No I'm not." Kara laid down as she argued. "You're the liar if you think I went to bed early after making us a bed in that sand dune."

***

Despite the early hour, Thrake talked incessantly about any topic that popped into his head as he climbed a few paces ahead of Aer and Kara. It was like he needed to make up for his lack of speech while gagged overnight. Or he was trying to kill them by sheer irritation.

As the headache at the base of her skull boomed, Aer wondered why she had shown him any mercy by removing his gag. Her name was supposed to be ironic.

"Kara, where's that damn cloth?"

"You took it out of his mouth, how should I know?" Kara hissed back. "I shut him up yesterday, it is your turn. And do it quick before I remove his head. Why can I not remove his head again?"

"I can't remember." Aer had a reason for not killing him before removing his ties; one she couldn't recall as she stared at his back.

At that moment the naiad turned around, smirking like she hadn't been contemplating bludgeoning him to death. Aer drew her sword. "Shut the hell up. You talk any more during this climb and I'm cutting out your tongue."

"Don't worry, baby doll," he crooned to her from above. "It'll grow back and I'll be able to show you all the things I know how to do with it."

He took a step towards her but stopped abruptly as he continued to look her in the eye. Aer cocked her head, unsure why he stopped. "Well, big guy. Come and show me then."

For just a moment it looked like anguish lit his eyes. Before Aer could say anything more, Kara threw a rock.

"Fwack, my nothse," he screamed as he clutched his face. Blood gushed out between his fingers as he bent over in pain. "Bichth."

With the moment broken it was easy for Aer to believe that she'd miss imagined his reaction. He was probably worried she was lulling him into a trap. Which she was. Aer high fived Kara. "Nice shot."

"Get moving, pig," Kara glowered at the male. He gave her a dirty look and started climbing again, muttering and shaking his head.

After a few hours, the group crested a plateau. "It's too hot for this," he whined as he sprawled out in the sunshine while the valkyries checked their surroundings.

Aer rolled her eyes and was about to tell him off when a flash of sunlight reflected off his chest. She moved in closer to inspect the medallion-like piece of jewelry around his neck.

Between his pectorals rested a solid piece of gold bordered by intertwined broad-faced leaves with a lotus etched at the bottom. A crossed mace and dagger were cut opposite the blossom, belying any sense of peace the flower might convey. In the centre, a crane stood in water, its arched-back head leading the eye to the topaz sun.

Almost unconsciously, the naiad lifted the piece by its gold chain and tucked it into his black t-shirt. Aer was about to ask him why he wore Hindu symbols when Kara interrupted.

"Something's over there." Kara nodded at a cluster of rocks that formed a high rise before the plateau turned into the wall of the mountain. Silently they approached, leaving Thrake behind. They drew their swords as they came closer to the form.

"Is someone there?" Kara called.

"Ný, open up," Thrake hollered directly behind them. Aer gritted her teeth and spun around to punch him in the gut.

"You ass, don't sneak up on me."

He may have wheezed a response while he clutched his middle that Aer didn't hear. She turned her attention back to the rocks, which now moved to reveal a tall elf standing in the middle of the opening. She wore a long purple gown that looked like it was made of silk, belted at the middle with a chain of silver teased by the tips of her auburn hair. She'd be beautiful if her brows didn't arch cruelly over her lapis eyes. Aer got the impression that the elf would walk daintily over her body after slitting her throat.

"Thrake, all of you should have been here yesterday." Aer and Kara turned their heads towards the nymph. "I told you to take them to the other gate. Megaera has been waiting."

Ný paused for an apology that never came. "What happened to your face?" Thrake had healed completely underneath the dried blood that flaked off his cheeks and chin. As soon as he opened his mouth, Ný held up a hand. "I take it back. I don't care. Come along, valkyries."

"I was only having a little fun," Thrake said as he scurried in behind the women before he could be locked out.

"Megaera likes him so he was given the task of guiding people to the gate. Nymph attention span is notoriously short and they're so easily distracted. I would rather have used a brownie, but what can you do?" Ný explained as she led them through a network of caverns. A barrage about the nuisance of naiads ensued as they walked. Thrake appeared like he didn't take offense while he mouthed the words along with the elf.

The requisite stalactites and stalagmites bordered the path they travelled as though they had been planted there like flowers, or moved aside by magic. A pleasant temperature surrounded the group, not cold or damp as would be expected. It had been a long time since Aer dwelled in an immortal's cave but she remembered them well from the days of her youth.

Ný brought them to the start of a long flight of stairs that seemed to descend to the heart of the mountain. In the distance Aer could hear voices.

"Are we heading straight to the summit?"

"Yes. Like I said, Megaera has been waiting for you."

Above her head, Aer could also hear the movement of water. "You wouldn't happen to have water for a shower here, would you?"

"There's a tub in your room," Ný said, looking her up and down. "You can clean up after the meeting."

When the elf was finished judging her and looked away, Aer checked to make sure she wasn't flashing undue amounts of cleavage. *Dammit.*

"Need someone to wash your back?" Thrake asked as he moved his hand like he was going to stroke her back. Except he changed his mind at the last second. Aer promptly swung her elbow into his face in response. His lip split and he swore.

"Don't worry, I'm very flexible." He swore again.

As they climbed down the stairs in single file, the distant voices grew steadily louder until Aer could decipher distinct words. Her hearing was exceptional so it was still a number of minutes before they entered a vast cavern filled to bursting with supernatural creatures. Valkyries, furies, and harpies made up the majority although Aer spotted giants, gnomes, a lone yeti, two wolves she hadn't seen in centuries, and a number of sorceresses she'd long been friendly with.

Still, the most eye catching feature stretched-out beneath her feet. The dining hall's sloped floor was laced with intricate veins that lead downward to a rectangular cut-out positioned before the high-table.

Ný showed the valkyries to empty seats at one of the long mess-tables before she and Thrake continued on. The first thing Aer and Kara did was grab steins from the centre of the table and down the contents. Water never tasted so good as far as Aer was concerned.

Across from them, their younger sisters Bryn and Róta smiled in greeting.

"I thought you two were in London," Kara said.

Bryn, who looked much like Kara with her golden-red hair, replied for the pair as she usually did. "Someone," she said cryptically, "owed us a favour."

"You wasted that on passage?"

Róta brushed back her loose blonde hair, a shade darker than Aer's own, to reveal the long scar that distorted the length of her face. Her lip quirked without mirth as she spoke, "What else is there to ask for now?"

"Honoured guests," Megaera's raspy voice carried from the high table. "Our final guests have arrived and you have all feasted. Now it is time to discuss why I have asked you to my stronghold."

Megaera, like most furies, wasn't very tall. She wore her black hair in the traditional style piled atop her head with bits of leather, metal, and feathers molding and shaping. The objects not only held the tresses together, they gave an illusion of height. The silver coronet circling her high forehead designated her position amongst the furies, as did her matching pair of wrist gauntlets encrusted with rubies. Breaking with tradition, the queen did not wear a choker around her throat as all her sisters did, which made the ragged scar over her voice box all the more visible.

"After the end began, I sent out messengers. They were told to go as far in every direction as they could and send immortals to this mountain. Here you are, picking up the pieces of your existences because of three inebriated tricksters."

Megaera did not rely on theatrics to gain the hearts and minds of those in her hall. She spoke regally from her central position at the raised table surrounded by high ranking furies and her favourites. Thrake sat up there, as did Ný.

"I collected you to do more than provide comforts, although I am sure this is the first time many of you have been able to eat your fill, drink, bathe, sleep on a bed." Megaera paused as the immortals took in the knowledge that they were now indebted to the furies.

"I will speak plainly. I want your aid in our attacks on Mount Olympus, Asgard, and Mount Kailash. The furies seek revenge on those who have so greatly wronged us, and those we call allies, now and in the past."

"Too long have those who rule us horded their power as gods and goddesses above, subjecting us to their constant whims and follies. Too long have they looked down their noses at us as nothing more than the fauna that lives amongst the ants.

"They have grown fat and soft in their thrones; unremarkable as humans turn their backs on them. Are we surprised this did not stop them from going too far?

We are prepared to make examples of Eris, Komos, Kali, and Loki where Zeus, Shiva, and Odin will not. Their families have ferreted them away like the vermin they are so that they cannot be harmed by ill-feeling immortals who have suffered from the apocalypses they've initiated."

Megaera let the reminder sink in before continuing. "Some still fear the wrath of the deities. Hence, the weasels continue to live. We have organization. We have numbers. We will not only be triumphant in slaying the guilty, we will show a united front to each pantheon. I cannot promise that a war is not in our future. What I can promise is that any notion of peace has gone the way of the earth.

"Yet," Megaera raised a hand to her heart, "I need a promise from you in turn. I need your oath that you are with us to the true end. Silence and loyalty are what I ask of you. Unity and retribution are what I have to offer."

Around Aer all the warrior races stood and cheered, some boisterously demanding where their oath-sealing blood needed to be spilt as they held daggers to their wrists. The valkyries in the cavern were some of the loudest –an organized attack was what they had been waiting for.

Creatures of the less violent races started murmuring and

their words reached Aer's sensitive ears. "What can us non-warring beings offer?"

"Gnomes don't fight."

"I don't know how to launch an attack on a fortress, does any peri?"

Megaera allowed the questions to go on for a moment before she raised a hand. The room hushed immediately. "We know that there are immortals present who are unused to the ravages of battle. We have other purposes for you. Anyone who cares for revenge shall be given the means to participate, from wil-o-wisp to mountain goblin, from vampire to succubus. We will need all of your talents for our plan. All of them. All you must do is take the oath."

As Megaera asked, everyone poised a knife at the ready over the wrist of their choosing and aimed for the tracks that laced the floor. Aer realized what an ingenious invention the veins were as one of the sorceresses at the high-table spoke the ancient rites. When the female asked them to spill their blood, Aer sliced deeply into her wrist. The welling crimson dripped healthily into the tracks in the floor before the wound healed.

Each and every immortal in the hall did the same. A few needed assistance, some covering their eyes while a more blood-thirsty neighbour sliced open skin for them. Still, all were ready to pledge their lives to make the guilty pay.

Aer paid no mind to the rhyming as the little hairs on the back of her neck rose while the sorceress invoked the magic to seal their oath. It felt as though invisible, scentless tendrils of smoke curled around the room, coming in from the halls that networked out from where they gathered.

Sorceress magic usually made most immortals nervous, but this gathering was beyond unusual. Everyone in the crowd held still with parted lips and starring eyes as they unconsciously leaned in Megaera's direction. Aer caught herself holding her breathe as she bit her lower lip. Even the blood magic being performed couldn't distract her from the excited emotions coursing through her.

As Aer's eyes followed the river of blood flowing in increasing speed towards the high-table, she located Thrake.

Nymphs were not a warring species, they avoided conflict at all costs. Yet, Thrake had needed no assistance cutting himself. Like the others beside him, he clutched a sharp dagger as a deep gash dripped blood directly into the basin that slowly filled with what the immortal's offered. The grim line of his mouth was the only detail that set him apart.

And the beautiful dagger, with its intricate pattern running up the silver blade in a curling mass of vines. The studded handle shone with topaz, like the medallion he wore. The weapon was definitely not designed for combat. It reminded her of the weapons they carried in a faraway sub-continent.

Everyone knew magic and silver were a no-go. *Is that naiad so stupid as to chance messing up his oath?*

The chanting of rites stopped, accompanied by a great tension that disappeared as soon as it was noticeable. The sealing of magic pulled Aer from her thoughts.

"I have one last item to share," Megaera rasped. "We have learned that the tricksters were pushed into their actions by a fourth party, and I do not speak of the bumbling Komos. Someone of much greater power spurred them on. We do not have an identity. We need the name."

***

"Goddess on high, this is risky," Kara hissed for the near-millionth time as she stood fidgeting beneath the portal to Asgard. Days ago, Megaera divided the most battle-hardened immortals in her chamber into three groups. A pair of furies directed each party, preparing them for the part they were to play and explaining how they were to storm the homes of the deities. They had intel from friendly gods and goddesses about where each target hid within their respective kingdoms.

Each team was assigned a palace and taught its points of weakness. Each team member was given a role and told how they were expected to carry out the mission. The three attacks needed to happen simultaneously so that the pantheons would not be forewarned and able to rally defences.

The only truly risky part in Aer's mind was the rushed

nature of their organization. The past few days were a blur aside from the important parts that had been drilled into their heads. Timing was critical now that there was a plan that could possibly leak out. And time was one of those uncontrollable bastards when he wanted to be, Aer knew.

"We've got this," Bryn said to no one in particular.

Aer was thankful her three sisters were with her, not that she was surprised they had been tasked with taking Loki's head. As valkyrie résumés went, theirs were long and bloody. The others on their team had equally impressive histories; from the cyclops, to the enormous grey wolf Varg, to the stout dwarf, most of them had ties to Asgard and bad blood with Loki.

Selena and Phaidra, their leaders, hadn't crossed paths with the troublemaker, and neither had the feathered harpy or the tiny gnome that joined them. Aer didn't care, bloodthirsty warriors were stellar additions, and the gnome was their secret weapon. His abilities with stone would be priceless in Asgard.

As for Thrake, Aer had no idea why he was there. One, Asgard was far from any body of water. Two, he was not allied with any of the immortals on her team. They had all threatened his life regularly during training. Three, he had nothing to add to the fight against Loki. He should have been assigned reconnaissance or mountain duty like the rest of the battle-unfit.

Besides, there was something off about him. His complexion was pale with dark shadows under his eyes, and his lips were chapped from him constantly biting them. Maybe the end was getting to his peaceful nature more than the rest of them. Except that explanation didn't seem to wash.

Plus, his behaviour was erratic. Despite his flirting, he never touched her. Not that she wanted him to. But naiads were the type to put up or shut up. Thrake talked too much and never made a move. All of it wasn't adding up to anything Aer understood.

Thrake bumped her shoulder with his as he edged Bryn away from her. Kara glared daggers at him from her other side. When Aer look over she realized he'd only touched her because he was fidgeting more than Kara.

"Everyone's in position," Selena said aloud. "He should

be opening the gate soon."

He being Heimdall, the guardian of Asgard and one of their insiders. As long as they didn't harm his masters Heimdall was willing to let the group in for Loki. It was never good to be on a guardian's bad side before you made a colossal ass of yourself in an attempt to prove your end was the worst end.

After a few anti-climactic moments where nothing happened save the cold north wind whistling around them, Thrake opened his mouth. "Well that gate opening was beyond words. I've seen more exciting entrances on old vampires."

"Do you ever shut up?" Kara asked. If there was a Naiad Fan Club, Kara was not a member. Aer wouldn't be surprised if she formed and headed an Anti-Thrake Committee.

"Nope, not even when I'm enjoying the throes." The nymph grinned.

"This is serious and not only are you talking non-fucking-stop but you are making jokes? We could be beheaded the moment we are transported up, you realize, yes?"

"Wild one, lighten up," Thrake said. "I'd help you relieve some tension if you'd only ask." He ducked as Kara threw a knife at him.

Before she could do anything more, the ground rumbled and the runes usually hidden within the stone they stood on erupted. Spiny ridges in impossible to decipher, interweaving patterns sprang up and their surroundings changed. Symbols remained under their feet as the transport completed, placing them in the centre of a room lined with smooth onyx. No discernible marks marred the sheets to show they were individual slabs. The stone merely curved upwards into a domed ceiling that gave way to a swirling mass of clouds that depicted scenes from Norse legends.

It had been over five centuries since Aer had stood in this hall, so obviously crafted by gods and goddesses. The beauty of Asgard was undeniable even while it made her cringe. She'd loved the place as a child, but as she'd grown into her immortality something in her had called out for adventure. When a much older Kara had come home and offered to take Aer with her on her next outing, she hadn't looked back. Standing beneath the dome only reminded her that soon she would return here permanently.

Heimdall cleared his throat from the sole exit out of the chamber. As one the group swung to face him.

Aer studied his pocked face with its skin tan and ruddy from many journeys over blinding ice. He stood seven feet tall in magnificent, hand-casted gold armour, specially moulded for him because his shoulders were the width of a barn. A broadsword hung off one hip and an axe the other, both beautiful pieces of metal-work.

There was welcome in his eyes, so Aer threw herself at him just as she had on the day she left. Heimdall's smile disappeared when he put her down. "Go down the south path and follow it beyond the atrium. You will pass the servants' suite of rooms and come to an alabaster wall. You know the password. He is in there."

"The servants will not go to the king?" Kara asked.

"I have given them express commands to look at no one who may go down those halls."

"We are sorry to bring you to this treachery, Heimdall," Aer said. The other valkyries expressed similar feelings.

"You did not, he brought this upon himself," the guardian replied. "Be careful, maidens."

"We always are," the valkyries chimed as one.

Aer waved the other immortals forward and then jumped up to place a kiss on Heimdall's cheek. "Take care, giant." He blushed as her sisters followed suit.

Turning serious, she spoke quietly as they headed down the main path. "Whatever happens, no one is to say *his* name, the O-word, or the T-word, unless we want the entire palace to come down on our heads."

"I would recommend we say no names," Kara chimed in. "These walls have sensitive ears and long memories."

"True enough," Róta murmured.

"Remember the incident with so and so and the dragon? Nightmare and a half," Bryn said.

The valkyries chatted as they followed the path. The other immortals remained silent, listening to their talk and taking in the grandeur of the halls. The idea was to look like they belonged. Aer hoped they were successful as men and women passed by.

Thrake sidled up to Aer. "It's beautiful here. Why would you ever leave?"

"I am not a goddess, handmaid, or advisor. The valkyrie is a creature of adventure, battle, and carnage. Those things do not make it up here, thankfully, so we must search them out." Aer sighed, "At least, that's what we used to do. After this, I don't know."

Before the naiad could say anything, the party arrived at the alabaster wall and Kara called Aer forward. Bryn spoke the password since she had been in Asgard most recently. Even in these heavenly halls passwords changed routinely, just not often by mortal standards.

The stone split smoothly and a hallway arched with slate opened before them. "Ready?" Selena whispered. Once they crossed this threshold there was no going back.

Ornate archways lined the walls, each opening into massive chambers that housed decadent furnishings for sensual lounging. Aer and Kara had become the leaders and they ducked their heads inside of each room to check for occupants. They each took one side of the hall and signalled to the others while they advanced.

Nearly fifty yards from where they started, Aer saw Loki. He lay back on a chaise lounge with his back to her, distracted by the dancing of a graceful woman wearing nothing but layered scarves. Scarves she was removing one by one as her hips swayed to the slow tattoo drummed out by another woman sitting a little ways behind her. She was dressed in scarves as well and smiled dreamily at the god.

Aer ducked back into the hall. Loki's head was being hunted and he allowed himself to be distracted. She could believe it.

She signalled to the group and most readied themselves by pulling various blades from sheathes. As per their plan, Varg moved into the main position as he would be the one to neutralize Loki.

When he nodded his massive grey head, they entered the

chamber at a run. The drummer noticed them first and let out a squeal. Phaidra ran at the maiden and smashed her in the temple with the hilt of her sword. She fell in a heap over her drum.

The dancer ran to Loki for protection but he shoved her away from him as he turned around to face the force threatening him. Loki took them in with a superior grin until Varg tackled him with a running leap, grabbing him around the midriff with huge jaws and taking him to the marble floor with a thud.

Bryn took care of the dancer, pinching a vein in her neck that made her pass out instantly. No one caught her as she fell to the floor.

The group stood back as Varg and Loki wrestled on the floor. The wolf's snapping jaws looked strong enough to crush steel, yet the god had a few tricks and blades up his sleeves. The wolf growled and shook the god every chance he got.

The fight ended when the wolf head-butted Loki in the nose. Blood drenched them both as Varg took the advantage and flipped a groaning Loki onto his stomach. Thrake came in from the side and took over the wolf's position. He fisted the god's dark hair and smashed his forehead into the stone ground until he stopped squirming, still conscious. Thrake pulled out that beautiful dagger without releasing Loki's hair.

"Who put you up to it?" Thrake demanded.

"I don't know what you're talking about." A bead of blood welled up from the small slice the naiad made on his throat.

"You would die in another's place? That sure doesn't sound like the Loki of legend."

"I'm sure I don't have a clue what you're going on about." Smash went his forehead onto the floor again.

"Enough," Kara said. "We're out of time." She moved into position to remove the god's head with her sharp broadsword. While Megaera wanted the identity of the mastermind, she knew there were other ways to uncover it than letting the three deities live.

Just as Kara raised her blade to swing, she was launched across the room. She hit the wall and landed in a clattering heap of mail and sword. Aer blinked slowly, unable to comprehend what had happened as the naiad straightened out of the stance that allowed him to roundhouse kick her sister.

"I have to tell you there's been a change of plans," he said in a monotone. As though waiting for the words, a mix of male and female water nymphs and reptilian naganis flashed into the chamber.

Outnumbered, the raiding party jumped into action. Aer didn't know how the others fared as she was rushed, and didn't have time to care. She slashed and hacked at the creatures around her. Despite her preternatural speed and skill she couldn't seem to kill them as they overwhelmed her.

She cursed as a nagani and nymph assaulted her blade in tandem with two of their own. Someone kicked her in the back, sending her flying toward her enemies. The grip on her sword loosened and she took a fist to the mouth. Spitting blood, she made as though to renew her attack when she felt three sword tips jab her neck. Aer dropped her blade and raised her hands, grinding her molars.

The attackers had their entire group disarmed –some pinned to the ground, others merely held at sword point. Selena and the harpy lay unconscious and bled freely onto the floor while Phaidra stood over them. Varg lay unconscious, too, his tongue lolling on the ground. Multiple swords punctured his big body. The gnome flailed in the arms of a single blue-scaled nagani who held him high above the floor, effectively nulling his power over the stone he needed to touch to manipulate. The giant looked dead. All four valkyries stood with hands in the air, each with no less than three blades held at their throats.

Aer's lip throbbed with every beat of her heart and she panted even though she was no longer exerting herself. She felt hot and cold at the same time as she fought the need to scream fuck it and tear into the creatures before her with her bare hands. She narrowed her eyes at the treacherous bastard still standing over Loki. "You disgusting son of a bitch."

"I'm sorry, baby doll," Thrake said. "All's fair in war, right?"

"Fuck you," Aer spat. She swatted at the sword touching her throat. "Get that out of my face."

The naiad whose sword she hit slapped the side of her head with the flat of his blade. "Behave yourself." One of the other males securing her chuckled under his breath. Aer kicked out backwards like a mule and heard him thump to the ground, sucking air through his teeth.

She smirked, and the naiad in front of her slugged her without warning. She stumbled back hard.

"Enough," Thrake decreed as he walked towards them.

Aer wiped the blood from her split lip with the back of a hand, returning to her former position. Thrake glared at his fellows and they backed off from her. He had the nerve to look at her with concern as he approached. *What the fuck is his deal?*

When he was within reach she punched him with everything she had. He landed on his ass a good two feet from her. "Stay away from me."

The naiad opened his mouth to speak then promptly closed it, looking past Aer. When she heard a rustle behind her, she turned her head. A tall woman stood before the entrance the gnome had sealed shut. She glanced at the disarrayed creatures, her haughty expression scalding. Aer had been around a lot of deities in her time, never had she felt such power emanate from someone who looked on her fellow immortals like they were cockroaches in need of extermination.

The woman moved towards Loki and the naiad that still held him. The saffron yellow dress she wore swirled about her ankles as she strode forward, providing glimpses of the golden pants that hugged her calves. Her hips swayed even though she wore flat soled slippers, reminding Aer of the only tiger she'd ever encountered in the wild. The bodice's long sleeves were trimmed with gold beads and tiny crystal prisms that flashed blinding light. As she passed by Aer, a musky smell wafted from her, like wet, rotting leaves and stagnant water. As Aer's sinuses tingled, she realized it was the same scent Thrake had carried when she tied him up on Antofalla.

Standing before Loki, the woman flipped her hair, the dark sheet mesmerizing as it swayed down her back. Abruptly, she spun on her heel to face the room. The bindi between her maroon eyes glimmered as only genuine topaz would and gold jewellery adorned her ears and fingers. The yellow and gold called Thrake's jewellery to mind.

"Thrake, I cannot decide if you are brilliantly daring or stupidly lucky." He stood up in a rush and bowed in the direction of the woman; the other naiads and naganis did likewise. "You were nearly too late, Thrake. He nearly lost his head." The softness of her tone made Aer flinch even though she wasn't the one being addressed.

"My apologies, Bagala."

Aer found Kara's eyes across the room. *The Hindu goddess of justice? The one who disappeared millennia ago? She's the mastermind behind the end?*

Aer's confusion only grew as she turned back to watch the goddess. No justice deity she had ever met glowed with an aura that exuded this manic menace, one that made an immortal afraid to breathe in case the creature before them took it as a challenge.

"I've found you useful so far, Thrake. You do not want that opinion changed."

"What is going on here?" Phaidra hollered from the back of the room. A grunt followed her outburst. It went against the grain but Aer was thankful to whoever had moved to silence the fury. If the group stayed quiet they might make it out in whole pieces.

Contempt lifted the corners of Bagala's red-painted mouth. "I can't have those who are keeping my apocalypses active harmed."

"I should have removed his head when I had the chance," Kara muttered.

"It would have been the intelligent thing to do," Bagala nodded. "But none of you did, and now all of my tools are safe in my hands."

"You'll be stopped, you crooked bitch," Kara taunted.

"You dare threaten me?" Bagala screamed as the topaz jewel on her brow swelled and her breathing grew heavy. The tension in the chamber made Aer's skin crawl as the woman clenched and unclenched her fists and jaw. The struggle seemed to go on for an age before the topaz split and a lightning blue iris flashed.

"Shiva dallies too long with his consort while the world festers, so mutated by lies that it is an ugly, twisted shadow of what it once was. Truth and lie, deceit and honesty, treachery and loyalty –it's all the same and not the same. I *will* fix it." Bagala inhaled deeply and the third eye closed. She smirked and turned away like she'd never lost control, twitching her hair again.

Right, Aer thought, *she's bat-shit crazy.*

"Thrake, help Troy," Bagala commanded. Before complying, Thrake looked unblinkingly at Aer as though trying to transmit thoughts from his brain to hers. She only hoped she successfully conveyed every bit of the hate she felt.

"Yes, Bagala," he said and turned away. Aer raised her chin.

"You know where to take him," Bagala said. "You can leave these ones alive for now. Obviously, they are not the threat they hoped to be."

Aer ground her teeth at the insult as Bagala disappeared as spontaneously as she had arrived. Still, it was what she'd hoped for.

"Sorry to ruin your plans, but our mistress has further use for this one," Troy, who could easily pass for Thrake's lighter haired bother, said as he kicked Loki in the side. He grabbed one of the god's arms and waited for Thrake to grab the other while Loki flopped around. "And she's a helluva lot scarier than the likes of you guys."

One of the naganis near Aer pulled an amulet out of her shirt identical to Thrake's. Aer flushed, feeling like a novice idiot for not putting the pieces together about the treacherous nymph. Now all she could do was stand with her arms raised as the attackers readied to transport the god.

Why would someone like Thrake mix with the likes of Bagala? She'd heard the naiad queen, Edessa, was a merciless shrew who'd do anything to bring her race to glory. Perhaps siding with the water deity was the queen's means of finally doing so.

Not that that gave Thrake an out. Aer didn't care if he'd been ordered to betray their party by the psychotic nutcase or not.

He'd taken an oath and broken it. Oh, and he aided those who brought about the end. He wasn't going to get away with it as long as she still had her head.

Thrake was staring at her again as he held Loki's other arm. "Begin," he said, and the slimy reptile with the amulet started chanting.

I had to, Thrake mouthed at her. His usual playfulness was gone, replaced by a lacklustre determination. She showed him her teeth in aggression.

Your head is mine, Aer mouthed. Thrake nodded once.

As Bagala's minions flashed Loki away, Aer couldn't stop the smile that stretched her cheeks to the point of discomfort. She put her hands on her hips and looked at her bloodied team. Yes, they'd failed spectacularly. Still, she sensed victory in the air.

Not only did she have a new adventure to devote herself to, Megaera was going to be very pleased to have that name. Plus, Bagala wanted the three alive, which meant that Megaera's army might just be able to stop these apocalypses before earth was irreparably totaled.

Vindication

Nina Waters

Her screams were starting to grate on my nerves.

I briefly considered helping her, just so that she'd be quiet, but my sense of self-preservation was stronger than the faint sense of duty that suggested that maybe I should intervene. Instead, I pointedly ignored her cries, the crackling of the fire, the shouts of the furious mob assaulting her, as I went about my business. If I acknowledged what was happening, I would be expected to join in. My depravity might run deep, but even I had qualms about participating in the burning of one of my own People.

There lay the crux of the problem. Intervene, save one of a dying People. Intervene, and risk exposing my unscarred face. Intervene, and most likely end up dead right alongside her. It was her own fault for getting caught, I justified, with our powers only the foolish should be discovered by humanity. I hadn't thought any of the foolish were still alive.

The sounds were starting to fade behind me as I walked hurriedly, when suddenly her incoherent shrieks resolved into words that I could understand.

"I'm not one of them!" desperate and choking, all of her energy seemed to go into making herself intelligible. "I'm not a Fae! Please don't do this! Please…" Her word faded off into sobs, and then was drowned out by a roar from the crowd.

She had said enough. I stopped. The humans would expect one of us to say that, to say anything to save themselves, but I knew better. One of my People wouldn't try to save themselves through denial - it never worked. They would instead use every trick at their disposal to try to escape. Yet, I realized

I'd neither seen nor sensed any spells. No illusions, no sonic booms, no mass confusion - just myself on a narrow deserted street lit by the flickering of the fire light in the square, humming with the roar of the crowd, reeking with the smell of burning wood and plastic and who knew what else.

If she really wasn't a Fae, why would they think she was? Our only distinguishing feature was our unblemished skin. She must not have any scars, and if she didn't, that meant she wasn't infected. If she wasn't infected...the ramifications were mind boggling. Could a human actually be immune? I'd looked all over the world, travelled to the most dismal, distant, isolated locations on the mere rumor that such a human might exist, and had always come up empty handed. There was no such thing. There was no escape. There wasn't a human alive who didn't have the Blight; soon there would not be a human alive. If there was even a chance that she was human and wasn't afflicted, I had to act. I had to save her. I had to know what made her different.

I ran to the nearest building entry and pulled it open. The old elevator shaft in the dusty, cobwebbed lobby was nothing but a gaping hole into a black abyss, and the light bulbs, last electrified who-knew-when, were all shattered, but the stairs were undamaged, and I ran up them two at a time. The scarf I used to hide my features fell away, and a pile of rags that I had mistaken for trash screamed as I ran by with my fair face literally aglow, but I couldn't spare the time to care. Secrecy was pointless now.

The door to the roof was chained shut, but I was awash in power. I injected pure chaos into the carefully aligned bonds and atoms of the metal and the door dissolved in a swirl of energy. From the roof, I could see the entire square. The bonfire was built out of whatever flammable rubble and old furniture the mob could find. Atop the burning refuse heap was my screaming damsel in distress, her clothing aflame, a faint hint of burning flesh mingling with the noxious fumes of plastics and synthetics burning. In the flicker of the firelight she didn't look any less scarred than the scores who mobbed her, her face contorted by agony, terror, sweat and soot as theirs were twisted and deformed by the Blight that would kill them all.

There was no time to plan, no time to consider, no time to

be prudent. She was my last chance, my only chance to find a cure. I couldn't let her die. Clouds spontaneously filled what had been a brilliantly clear twilight sky, and rain began to fall, briefly as a drizzle, briefly as a steady pitter-patter, briefly as sheets, and then the very air seemed to become water. The flames doused instantly, and few of the humans were strong enough to stand under that onslaught. My skin felt like I was the one afire; it had been generations since I had attempted something this difficult. A crystal staircase formed before me, leading from the roof to the top of the extinguished pyre, and I did my best to traipse down the stairs. Make it look easy, make it look effortless. Remind the humans of the power that they meddled with when they attacked my People. The woman was tied to a post in the center of the bonfire, the ropes all that kept her from collapsing.

No time. I grabbed her arm and dragged her behind as she whimpered, dissolving the ropes into nothing. I cloaked us in invisibility and silence as I pulled her up the stairs. An illusion of myself remained where I had last appeared, haranguing the prostrate humans about the folly of their ways. My mind started to feel like it was being torn apart, too many active spells, to many things to keep track off. The rain flickered in and out of existence between droplets. The stairs disintegrated behind us as we reached the roof. My hands shook as the rain died away completely and the illusion of me faded. Desperately, I clung to our invisibility, our only bastion of safety, as I looked around the roof for any shelter, any protection. There was a water tower, old and battered and long since abandoned. I opened a hole in the base of the tower and we climbed in. I sealed it behind us. Exhaustion overcame me, my strength gave out, and I fell on my face, enveloped in blackness. Maybe I'll never wake up. Then all this would be someone else's problem. I didn't mean the spectacle I'd just put on.

***

Faint daylight filtered through the damaged roof of the water tower when I finally opened my eyes. My prize lay sprawled opposite me, watching warily; when she saw that I was awake, she began to weep, tears forging fresh trails down her filthy face. She tried to get as far away from me as she could, pressing herself against the side of the tower. A piece of her charred clothing crumbling to dust, revealing mottled red skin, cracked and bleeding.

"Oh, please," I said, shocking myself with how hoarse and scratchy my voice sounded, "stop that."

"Are you going to kill me?" she asked pathetically.

Had she really spent untold hours curled opposite my unconscious form just waiting to find out if I was going to kill her when and if I woke up? "Of course. That's what my People do. I risked my life and rescued you entirely so that I could kill you myself."

Instead of laughing, she looked even more frightened. "My momma told me that your People want to kill us all. She told me you gave us the Blight."

"Well, that part is true. We did give you the Blight. But if I had wanted you dead, I would have just left you in that fire. If you thought I was going to kill you, why did you just wait here?"

"You might have been faking."

I laughed. In the shadowed darkness, I could finally actually look at her. She was young, I realized, maybe not even a teenager yet, and there was an angelic look to her. What was left of her hair was blond, and her features were pale, eyes blue, pinched in pain from her injuries. And not a single scar. "I'm not going to kill you, girl. My name is Alliana, and I think that, together, we might be able to save the world." She gazed at me in amazement. "Are you really not sick?"

She nodded. "I've never had the sickness. I did get real sick a few years ago, momma said it was the flu. I didn't know that people got sick from anything else, I thought I was going to die. I didn't, I got better. And then momma died, and then Lou, and Raquel said she'd keep me safe but those people yesterday killed her, so now there's only me." She started to weep again.

Tiresome brat. Humans wasted so much time on things that didn't matter. "What's your name?"

"Sarah," she swallowed and hiccoughed.

"Take my hand, Sarah," I held mine out, trying and nearly

failing to keep it from shaking. Last night - or had it been longer than that? - had really taken it out of me. Tentatively, the child took my hand, and I used the type of magic that had always been my specialty - a perfect understanding of the unique interrelationships between the chaotic forces that enabled a human to function, to live. Humans had always intrigued me, even in my oldest memories I wanted more than anything to understand how they worked. Their bodies, so similar to our own, yet functioning without any magic whatsoever, it was the most remarkable thing I could imagine. I had disassembled many of them before I truly understood how it worked, how the parts functioned and interacted with each other, but the study had been worth it. I knew more about these strangely fragile, strangely resilient creatures than anyone else among my People. It was why I was still alive; I had always taken them seriously, appreciated the threat they represented, even as my kinsfolk played their power games and used humans as pawns and toys.

Even in my exhausted state, healing her should be easy. Interlacing my fingers with hers, I attuned myself to the energies of the cells and molecules busily at work within her body…and I found nothing. For a moment, panic seized me as a range of possibilities sprang to mind - she was a doppelgänger, she was a trap, I had burned out my magic - but then reason took over once more. She was clearly real, and nothing could burn out magical powers. To the best of my knowledge, there was no Fae left alive who could make such an impressive golem, and if there were, her owner would have been nearby, and I knew for certain I was the only Fae in the city. Could it be that she was immune to magic? Such an immunity would protect her from the Blight, but I would never have imagined that such a thing was possible.

"What are you doing?" she asked, sounding more curious than afraid.

"Nothing," I replied, dropping her hand. "Do you think you can stand?"

"Do I have to?"

"Yes."

"Then I will," and suiting actions to words, she forced herself to her feet, leaning against the slanted side of the water tower. Her expression was more pained than it had been, and most of her remaining clothing fell to ashes around her, but she was up. Her legs were badly burned, but the rest of her seemed mostly unhurt. I had gotten to her in time. I couldn't heal her magically, and there were no human hospitals left within a hundred miles, but I thought she'd survive. I forced myself to stand as if it wasn't one of the hardest things I'd ever done. If she could stand, hurt as she was, so could I.

Leaning down, I put a hand on the base of the tower, and opened the bottom once more, doing my best to ignore the wave of nausea that threatened to overwhelm me. "Wait here," I managed. Wrapping my shawl back around my head and face, I dropped out onto the roof. The bright sunlight stung my eyes, and I blinked back tears as they adjusted, hoping no one saw me in my helpless state. When my vision cleared, and I was relieved to see that the roof was empty.

"I think all the people are gone now," called Sarah in a half whisper. "It was really noisy for a while, but then it got quiet. I was a good girl, I didn't make a sound."

I sighed. She could have told me that earlier, but I also could have asked. I was being inattentive to details, and if I couldn't get it together I was going to get us both killed. "You did well," humans cared about praise like that, I'd learned. "You can come out now."

She climbed down and stood behind me, blinking. I considered our options. The remains of the bonfire were still visible in the center of the square below. A few people passed by, pointedly ignoring the ash that the wind swirled about them. Going down into the streets risked drawing attention. This rooftop abutted two others, though, close enough to walk from one to the next. We could bypass a lot of trouble on the ground level by simply going where the roofs led us. On one, I found some ancient laundry, hung out to dry in the sun ages ago, that provided a somewhat sodden, once-white sheet to drape around Sarah and hide her injuries and flawless complexion. She grimaced when it brushed her burns, but she didn't complain, wrapping it tightly about herself, draping her whole body in its folds, covering her hair and face, everything but her eyes. They gathered the light and gleamed a deep blue.

Eventually, our roof top highway ended in a 20 foot gap, a street running below. We'd made it around a mile from our starting point. Surprisingly, the roof door on the building was unbarred, and we were able to make our way downstairs. This building was not as well preserved as the last had been; the doors to what had once been nice apartments had been hacked open with axes, and the musty smell of a tomb pervaded the halls. No one would live in a building like this any longer, no one would even enter it. The doors to the street would be marked with a large red X, the mark of a building that had been searched and no survivors found. That made it perfect for my current need.

"Are you hungry?" I asked Sarah. She nodded, and followed it up with a huge yawn.

"I don't like it here," she said.

"No one will find us, and there will likely be some food for you, and a place to sleep - maybe even a bed. I bet we can find you a less disgusting sheet, too," I added, hoping to entice her. I couldn't see her face to know her reaction, but she followed me as I started to search apartments. I didn't much care if she agreed with me, as long as she did as I said.

It took a few tries to find an apartment with some cans of food, a sofa with mismatched cushions, and no corpses. Judging by the decomposition, these had been early victims, perhaps 5 years ago. It had happened like that, some whole buildings would get taken before the rest of the block was even infected. That hadn't been part of the original plan, and even with all that I had studied the plague I hadn't been able to determine why it had happened. It was one of the many constant reminders of just how little we had understood about what we were unleashing upon mankind.

* * *

As soon as she had eaten, Sarah fell asleep on the pull-out couch, and I took the opportunity to do a quick sweep of the rest of the building. It was 15 stories, and there was not a living human in it. I grew increasingly tentative as I got closer to the ground floor, but I needn't have been so concerned. When I got to the lobby I found that not only had the doors been chained shut and the glass painted over, but some overly paranoid - or optimistic - soul had actually welded them shut. This must have been a very early case; it had been a long time since anyone had the time or resources to do seal a building this completely, and it had been even longer since anyone was naive enough to think that would help prevent the spread of the Blight. I made my way back up to the top floor and, using a lock I had found in one of the apartments, I padlocked the roof access shut. I had been hoping to take Sarah out of the city, but with her injuries, we'd never make it undiscovered. A building like this was the next best thing. Enough food and water to stay for weeks, wait until things died down in the area, and do my research in peace. It was almost a dream come true, it was almost like having my laboratory back again. But nothing would reconstruct my meticulous research, my centuries of notes that had burned when my home was destroyed. I just had to do my best.

I stopped back at "home" to check on Sarah; she was sound asleep. Then, I went through the building again, gathering up the things I would need. It hadn't been looted extensively before being sealed, and though there was some evidence that others had found the unlocked roof access and carried off what they wanted, a remarkable amount remained. In an apartment inhabited by two mummified, gray-haired corpses, I found a collection of medical supplies, things a diabetic would have needed every day. In the next, hidden in the back of a closet I found a survival kit. The crate it was in was open, and next to it, a small body huddled in the corner still clutching the flashlight whose batteries had died ages ago. I grabbed the flashlight, put it back in the crate, and took the whole thing. Three apartments later, I even found D battery replacements. On and on I went, bypassing what I didn't need, collecting what I did, carrying it back up to our base camp in Apartment 15C. Five trips in, I was already exhausted as I lugged two reusable bags filled with three gallons of water and a whole lot of canned corn up four flights of stairs.

Sara was awake when I got there. "Do you need help?"

she asked. She shifted and whimpered, the skin on her legs cracking, pus leaking out. If she got an infection, she would die, and so would everyone else. Fortunately, my scavenging had found help for that, too.

"No, I don't," I set down the bags and pulled out a small blue jar with a white top, handing it to her. "Smear that over your burns, it will help. But make sure you don't use it all, it might be the only medicine we have, it needs to last if you're going to get better." She nodded mutely, opened the jar, and gingerly smeared some of the white salve inside over her injuries.

"It hurts," she said matter-of-factly. "Is it supposed to hurt?"

"Yes."

She nodded again, and kept at it. I got a can of food ready for her to eat when she was done, and then started to set up my new laboratory.

A fold up massage cot was my hospital bed; a coat rack held the closest thing to IV bags that I could find - colostomy pouches. The diabetic kit had been rigged into a system that I could use to take blood safely and store it in test tubes from a children's chemistry set, and an array of small personal electronics gave me at least a few options for analyses. I had never dreamed of meeting a human on whom I couldn't use magic, and it presented a myriad of challenges to my research that I had never faced before. Fortunately, curiosity had led me to learn a little bit about how humans went about doing medicine within their many limitations. I would manage. I had to.

"Are you hungry?" Sarah asked as I sorted through a clay tool kit for things I could use surgically, dropping the ones that I thought had a chance of functionality into a vase filled with peroxide. I hadn't noticed that she had finished with the healing balm and turned her attention to the cans of corn.

"No," I shook my head. "My People don't need to eat, not like you do."

"What do you eat?" She perked up, interested, excited. I suppressed a groan. "I remember once when I was a little girl, before the Blight came, momma took me to the zoo, and the different animals ate so many different things, the polar bears ate raw meat and the birds ate honey water and the anteater ate, you know, ants, and the monkeys, they didn't eat bananas and I was really upset because TV had told me that they would. I wonder what happened to the animals when the people got sick?"

"Are you suggesting that we eat the way animals eat?" She looked upset, and I smiled to show I wasn't actually upset. "You were lucky here - the animals stayed locked in their cages and had died before some idiot could come through and free them. Many other places weren't so lucky; there are prides of lions feasting on buffalo meat on the Great Plains, and the streets of Tampa are now hyenas' hunting ground." She looked troubled, so I tried to divert her attention by answering her original question. "We do need sustenance, but much less than you. And we prefer sugar. Honey is very popular, and maple syrup." What I wouldn't have given for some honey. Maybe I'd find some on the lower floors.

I wanted to get started studying her right away, but as I finished building my lab, and Sarah finished eating her corn, I found I didn't have the energy. There was so much I needed to explain to her, so much that I needed her cooperation for, but at the moment all I could think of was falling flat on my face. Denying it wasn't helping, and so I forced myself into acceptance. "Sarah, I need to sleep now. If you hear anything at all inside the building, even if you think it's just a rat, you wake me up right away, okay?"

"Yes, ma'am!"

***

When I woke up, Sarah was leafing through a book filled with colorful satellite images of Earth, the flashlight I had fixed the only light in the room, reflecting off the glass windows. "Turn that off!" I shouted, fully awake in an instant. She just blinked and stared at me. "Turn it off," I yelled again, "right now!" Hesitantly she did so, and the room plunged into darkness; out the window was a back alley, several windows showing the flickering of fire light. How could she have been so stupid? "If anyone saw that light, if anyone comes to investigate, they'll kill us! We have to move, leave here, right now!" We should leave the building completely, but I'd never find these resources again. We needed them.

"I'm sorry," she said tearfully. I crossed the room and smacked her across the face, sending her sprawling, leaving a red handprint across her cheek. "I'm sorry," she repeated brokenly.

We carried my makeshift lab down to the 13th floor and into an apartment across the building, with only faint red emergency lighting to help us find our way. If anyone came to investigate the electric light that they had seen - so rare now - we would at least have some warning if they started near where they'd first seen the light. The very first thing I did was cover the windows with layer upon layer of cloth. As I arranged the room to my liking, dumping the corpses of the family that once lived here into the hall, I lectured Sarah.

"From now on, don't do anything without asking me. Don't talk, don't eat, don't sleep. Check with me before you take a piss. Don't turn anything on or off, don't move anything. The only thing you should do without checking with me is wake me up if you hear anything suspicious. Do you understand?" We should change buildings. We should go elsewhere. We'd never find another place like this to hide. If I could use magic on her, it would be different, but I couldn't, and where would I find this much medical equipment ever again? Maybe with this lab, I could find the answer before people came to investigate. Maybe no one had seen. It might be safer here than trying to leave with Sarah so hurt. Even as common as fires were now, no one could mistake the source of her injuries. Time was running short. That thought rang loud and true in my head, though I didn't know why or what it meant. There wasn't enough time.

"Yes," she said miserably. There was a bruise on her cheek. "I'm sorry." She said again.

"Here's what we're going to be doing. You are immune to the Blight. For that reason, I am going to do medical tests on you and study you, in an effort to determine why you aren't infected. If I'm successful, I'll be able to come up with a cure for the disease, and save everyone. If I fail, everyone is going to die." She looked frightened, but she nodded determinedly.

"I want to help. I want to save everyone. Can we start now?"

***

It took another few days before I felt at all like myself. It would be a long time before I fully recovered, but at least I no longer needed to sleep. Those first days were very tense, wondering if every muffled sound was humans storming the building, but no intruders came. Sarah was still cowed, though I started to relent from my earlier burst of anger. I instructed her on how she could explore the building safely, and I spied on her to be sure she followed my directions. Once I knew she wouldn't get us caught, I let her take over foraging for her own food and water. The burns were healing, and she moved past the risk of infection, which could have caused an ironic end for one with her peculiar gift.

A week passed, and I was already making rapid progress. There was very little that I could really do with the equipment at hand, but luck was with me for once. Her blood was the key. I had made an extensive study of blood some centuries ago, passing an entertaining score of years collecting humans of every blood type, harvesting their blood. There had been a room in my house where the great glass-smith Omilin and I had collaborated; he had taken their drained bodies and made three dimensional glass molds, perfect, life-sized replicas of how they had appeared in life. I had poured all of their blood inside the vessels, and he had sealed them in vacuum, a gorgeous museum of the 30 main groups. It had been one of the gems of my collection. In all that time, I had never seen anything like Sarah's blood. She was something new, something unique. If I could just isolate what made her blood different, could I inoculate the other humans? I tried variation after variation, knowing that ultimately I'd need to capture some of the diseased people in order to test it, trying not to think about that stage of the process. Trying not to think about the magic immunity that I would be propagating along with that inoculation. After everything that had happened, everything I'd done, was I truly to be the Fae who rendered humans immune to our influences? What would the others say, if they ever found out? I had been loved, revered, respected amongst my People. If word of this ever got out, I would be reviled.

If I didn't cure the Blight, there would be no one left to revile me. All the humans would be dead, and they would have killed every single Fae on their way out. When the Blight had first struck, it was going to be our salvation. A world with no more humans in the way, their hatred so destructive, their rapidly growing web of iron and steel fencing us in to the few remaining wild places. The Blight was the cure to that slow doom, the world would be ours again. Without human maintenance, the iron would rust away, the cities would crumble, and the wilderness would spread. There were plenty of other species that were entertaining enough to while away our millennia. I imagined turning to the study of apes or sharks. When the Blight was first unleashed, we had hope. I attended to many celebrations, parties, galas and masques. For the first year a grand time was had by all, I couldn't remember when I'd last seen my People so happy.

The first Fae murders seemed an unfortunate but unavoidable consequence, and our spirits weren't dampened. But then more and more died, and it became clear that our immunity marked us like a banner. So accustomed to moving unnoticed through the crowds of mankind, we now stood out as the only beings not sick. We tried using magic to mimic the humans' sickened appearance, we attempted to use make up to replicate the scarring, but somehow, they always knew. Word got out that the Fae had created the Blight, some poor foolish Fae thinking that their life would be spared if they told what they knew. Even humans who had previously been content to live and let live now used their knowledge to bring us down. Those who had been graced to see our homes now led the hordes that destroyed them. Those who had entertained us with their antics now contrived to trap us and kill us. In trying to save ourselves, we had instead tied our end to theirs as surely as if we were the ones who suffered from the Blight. If I could find the cure, though, if a Fae were known to have undone what the Fae had once wrought, perhaps we might yet all be saved.

I had just isolated the protein in her blood cells that

activated when I tried to use magic on it when I heard a clatter on the staircase and Sarah came rushing in, out of breath from running up the stairs.

"Alliana!" she managed. I opened my mouth to tell her off, when I realized it was the first time she'd ever called me by name. "Alliana, there are people coming!"

"What did you see? Tell me everything!"

"They're gathering downstairs. I was looking out one of the windows a few stories up. The windows on the first floor are all boarded up, but there are some on the second and third that can be reached, they've leaned stuff against the building and when I saw them they were almost done. They'll be here any moment," the words came in a rush. "I recognized the one giving orders, he was Raquel's husband. He killed her when she said she wouldn't turn me in."

With a cry of rage at our discovery, I looked around quickly. Was there anything I could salvage? I poured the sample I had just been working on into an empty water bottle, even knowing that the unsterilized bottle might contaminate the blood. The sample represented a week's progress when every minute was precious. "Look out the window! Can you see them?" I shouted, over loud. Sarah bolted to the window.

"They're coming in! They're coming in through the windows," she sounded terrified. I couldn't blame her. She already knew what being burned at the stake felt like, whereas I wouldn't find out until they caught us. If I lived that long.

"Run, girl. Get up the stairs, the key for the padlock is in the bowl by the door, I'll follow." She was my most important sample. As long as she was alive, there was hope.

She bolted out the door as if the humans chasing her were in the room. Already, I could hear noise in the stair case. The humans were searching the building, but it would take them time, surely it would take them at least a little time. Distant crashes, the distinctive clamber of many feet on metal stairs and loud shouts echoed through the vacant halls.

The scream was louder than any of those noises. My blood went chill, and for an instant I froze, recalculating what I needed to take from the room. I knew with certainty that Sarah was dead. No more new samples would be available; I had to preserve what I had. Frantically, I gathered up what I could, pouring it into any vessel I might be able to carry without spilling.

"She came from this floor!"

"13th floor! We've got one of the Fae witches, let's find the other!"

I picked up an oxygen tank, the heaviest item I had to hand, and swung it with all my strength at the window. The window shattered, the cloth covering it whipped away, and within moments an arrow came through the opening. There were snipers on the roof across the street. That escape route was cut off. I turned around.

A man stood in my doorway. Above and in front of himself he held Sarah impaled on a spear, blood leaking from her mouth and from the wound. Her eyes were wide and already glassy with death.

"How stupid do you think we are?" he asked. "You think you can do what you did, and that we wouldn't find you? We always find you, blightless. And I can die happy knowing that I took one of you with me." He threw Sarah's corpse aside; she rested awkwardly on the ground with her limbs all askew like a broken doll. He reached to his belt and drew a gun. "I've saved this bullet since the day I got sick. 'Bill,' I told myself that day, 'one day you are gonna meet a fucking witch, and when you do, are you gonna burn it? Oh no, that just gives it time to escape. No, when I find one, I'm gonna shoot it.'" He cocked the gun, flipped the safety, and aimed at me. There was no more time, no place else for me to go. I was still too weak to do magic. "I've saved this bullet for four and a half years, just for you. You should feel honored."

Laughter bubbled out of me. I couldn't hold it in. I was the only one left trying to save their sorry, useless asses, and they'd killed Sarah, and now they were going to kill me. The blood samples I'd been working on mingled with Sarah's pooling on the floor. "That girl, she was your only hope," I managed between laughs. "Do you understand me? She was a human, you fucking idiot, she was completely human, she was more human than you'll ever be. She was the only one who could have saved you, and now she's dead." I couldn't hold it in, I doubled over, tears streaming from my eyes.

"What are you talking about?" He looked confused. I wondered why he hadn't shot me yet. Down the hallway, other humans were crowding in behind him, shouting questions, asking if the witch had been found. "All of you shut up!" He bellowed, and silence fell. "What do you mean?"

"I knew I was right about you humans all along," I wiped the tears off my face, but more fell, sobs mingling with my laughter. "Everything was crumbling, all of us were going to die, and I knew that I had found the answer - millennia of knowledge of how the human body worked turned to developing the perfect disease to end all of you. My crowning achievement, I, who had so long been derided and look down on by my fellows for my interest in what made humans function, finding the way to get rid of you once and for all. When I developed the Blight, I looked out at mankind, you pathetic, worthless lumps of skin and hate and lust, and I knew I'd found the answer, that you were too stupid to live, that you'd never be able to conquer your own base instincts, that you were so blind as a race that you were a danger to every other entity, sentient and otherwise, on this planet." The laughter was stilling now, the tears remained. "As the illness spread, and you fools took your deaths out on us, I'd come to wonder if I had been wrong. I became convinced that I had inadvertently unleashed our own doom when I had infected that first useless waste of carbon, hydrogen and oxygen. I regretted my choice, and I wanted to undo it, I sought the cure to the perfect, final solution that I had engineered. A hopeless task…until I found hope. But you just killed it." A fresh wave of laughter washed over me, I couldn't even talk. The gun wavered in his hand uncertainly. "You are too stupid, too cruel, too brutish. I was right all along. Well, come on, just fucking shoot me already. I fought it for so long, but maybe it was always going to end this way. I don't even care anymore. I just feel so vindicated. I was right all along. The Blight. My most beautiful creation."

The last thing I ever heard was my own laughter as the

bullet struck me in the chest.

Walkabout

Joyce Chng

He saw them even before they reached his table.

Idly, he poked at the tender lamb tagine, savoring the aroma and enjoying the assorted sensory pleasures a leisurely walk could bring. He wasn't neglecting his duties, just enjoying a brief respite and indulging in his favorite pastime: people-watching.

They walked up to his table, two women with dusky skin and slender limbs. One was taller and muscular. A glance at her would convince someone into believing that she was a body builder or an avid sportswoman. Her smaller companion smiled easily and had green kohl-ed eyes that gleamed with an inner amusement. They were both wearing casuals – t-shirts, pink blouse and a flowery skirt for the petite woman. Two women out on a shopping trip in the streets of Morocco. They wore scarves too, covering their heads, to respect the customs and the traditions of the land. The scarves were colourfully patterned at the edges, yellow star-shaped flowers for the petite half of the pair, vivid orange flame petals for the larger woman.

He waved to the waiter who brought two more wine glasses to the table. Without a word, they sat on the empty metal chairs around the table. The petite woman reached over and picked the wine bottle up gingerly, sniffing at it.

"Not the best kind of wine," she said and her voice was low, husky with a hint of a ready laugh. "You have had better."

He shrugged and swirled the dark red liquid in his glass. "Still drinkable, to say the least."

"They are looking around for you," the muscular woman added. "You are missed, you know."

He smiled and forked a cube of tender lamb from the tagine. It was fruity with apricots, citrus and raisins. It reminded him of the apricot grove in one of his temples. "I am not technically gone-gone, per se. I needed to just walk around."

The muscular woman smiled, a lioness's smile. "Well, walking in this form has its privileges."

"Ah, Sekhmet, my sister, there, you answered your own questions," he washed the lamb down with the wine. It was tart to the tongue, but as he said, drinkable. Not the best, but drinkable. He turned to the smaller woman beside her taller companion. "And you, Bast, you will probably enjoy Morocco."

"As I did, countless times, with the sistrum and lyre," she replied back, raising her glass in a silent toast. "It has changed a lot."

"Our people have changed a lot too," he pointed out. "Lamb tagine? It has apricots."

They both shook their heads. Politeness, such decorum. From Sekhmet, even. He lifted an eyebrow.

"Suit yourself," he sipped at the wine again, leaning back. The throngs of people moved like a river, like the Nile. Voices, sounds, smells – wonderful. He relished it.

"Remember your duties," Sekhmet reminded him. Even in this current form, her power seeped through, bright like a star. She would be the One going into battle with a laugh and a roar, her khopesh in her hand.

"Not going to forget," he saluted her with his wine glass.

"You are not the forgetting type, my dear brother. There is some…trouble."

"Then I will return, never fear."

He nodded, letting his real Self out a little, a bit of his power. His eyes gleamed amber. He was Yinepu. He would never forget.

***

It was not to say that Duat was a boring place. It was his domain, his land. It was terrifying to the ones who followed him, who saw him as Netjeru – it was a place of after-death and justice, where their sins were weighted, where souls were fed to the Beast. But his duty could be monotonous, at times. Routine to the stage that he founded it tedious. Hence, his walkabouts in his other favoured form.

Therefore, when he returned, he was taken aback by the news of a new sickness running through the land. The trip to Morocco had been a blessed trip, somewhat out of a peaceful dream, deeply restorative. Beyond Duat, a rare and hateful sickness lurked, hunted and ate up souls. Bast and Sekhmet warned him, didn't they? They came, specifically, to look for him; Sekhmet wasn't even the type who liked walkabouts in human guise. Of course except that one time when she got drunk with Bast eating chocolate cake melts liberally doused with whisky. He often poked fun at her secret love for alcoholic confectionary.

With his eyes, he could see that the sickness had a darkness in its heart. Sicknesses were often live creatures, a twisted blend of thought-forms and real body cells. Someone out there wanted people to hurt, to weep and to die. Someone hateful, filled with bile and spite. This darkness-sickness had arms reaching outwards. People were moving often these days, across the lands and the seas. They brought the darkness into other places. They brought the darkness into their own homes. Dark, dark gifts indeed.

Now Duat pulsed with signs of that darkness, indications of black hearts dotting the land like contagious disease on grape leaves. There were more deaths, more souls trying to leave the land of the living. This time, the souls were both the sinless and sinful. The darkness did not discriminate. Death did not discriminate.

For the first time in millennia, Yinepu felt the cold wind of something frightening on his back.

***

Of course, he was not going to be idle about it. He was never idle and never liked the idea of keeping still, always walking along the boundaries of life and death, always walking in cities and villages. He was going to pay a follower of his a social call.

Fenix Lee was an accomplished embalmer. In a country adverse to the ways of dying and the dead, and grappling with the consequences of an aging population, she was one of the rare few women who became embalmers. Her father ran funeral services ranging from Buddhist rites to Christian wakes. He was that open-minded. As for Fenix, she abandoned her medical career and turned to embalming instead.

Her hands were chest-deep in an elderly woman when the dark shape solidified before her and a man stepped forward, handsome and jaunty. He was dressed in a black suit and pants; she swore she saw stars swirling across the fabric. Even his shoes were stylish, polished to an obsidian shine.

The elderly lady had come from the hospital morgue in the early hours of the morning. Her flesh was still cold, locked in rigor mortis, with a smile on her blue lips. Fenix respectfully treated the organs with preservatives. The elderly lady had lung cancer which spread to the liver, and had suffered for a long time. The death was a relief for her soul and her family. May she live well in the land of the dead.

Fenix also knew that her bones, when cremated, would be blackened by the amount of drugs she had taken to stem the predation of the cancerous cells. But you couldn't stop predators. It was in their nature to hunt and kill.

Yet she wasn't prepared for the appearance of the strange man in the middle of the morgue.

"How did you get in?" she demanded. The morgue was restricted.

"Fenix, can you not recognize your lord?" the man said with a creamy voice. For a moment, the air shivered, a heat mirage, and Fenix glimpsed a jackal head, alert ears swivelled forward.

Her bloody gloved hands flew to her mouth. She ignored it, feeling only the shock and elation that shot through her body. It had always been a head-thing, her praise of and for Yinepu, lord of the dead. Her personal beliefs flew against her Taoist upbringing, simply because they came from the land of the

Blessed. They were not so different actually, if you distilled them into their purest essence. She had a statue of Yinepu at home, tucked in a corner of her tiny room. She often lit incense before it. It had always been a head-thing.

Now the head-thing, the theory-thing, had become real.

"Dua Yinepu," she whispered, her throat had constricted. Now she had seen him, she felt too the otherworldliness of him. The thinning of the realms, like pulled skin. She had joined a coven in her teens, but she soon left. Teenagers were teenagers, too excited and ungrounded. She picked up the skills and lessons on her own. Piercing the veil was one of them.

The man in the black suit and pants smiled, a jackal smile. "Fenix, I apologize if I startled you at your holy task. But urgent matters press upon us. I need to speak to you."

***

The new illness sweeping across Asia, the Middle East and Europe was called Darkness. In scientific terms, it belonged to the family of coronaviruses like SARS. In deadliness, it surpassed even SARS. Every country in the world scrambled to cushion the shock, to protect their people. Every country had their patient zero. SARS mowed down people across the ages. Darkness scythed through them like ripe wheat.

When it infected an American man coming back from his business trip to Dubai, Darkness found an open gateway and strode in boldly like a conqueror backed by might.

News agencies across the world were already calling it an apocalypse.

***

"There is a sickness in the land," Yinepu explained. "A sickness like darkness. The land of the dead cries with the recently-deceased souls, shocked out of their bodies by this hateful thing. Have you seen it yet?"

By then, Fenix had sewn up the elderly woman's body and clothed her in the clean blue samfoo and black pants provided by her family. The wake was scheduled later in the morning and her father was due to deliver the coffin in an hour's time.

"I have heard… reports on the news," Fenix said, washing her hands with antiseptic soap at the morgue's sink. "There are some cases here." She had seen the news, heard the prosaic "Do not be alarmed" reassurances from the media. They were lying. She had felt something pressing against her consciousness. A warning, surely.

"The cases will increase. Thousand-fold, my child."

Fenix tilted her head. She was a small bird-like woman, small-boned and quiet. "Why me, lord?"

"Because you, my child, are one follower I can easily trace. Others, too many by lip service."

"I am sorry, lord. I thought with the revival of Kemeticism, your followers would grow. We still need the Netjeru." *But do you need us?* That thought came out from nowhere and scared her. *Why did I think that?*

"I am not sure if the Darkness is the work of Set," Yinepu continued, admiring the place. Human morgues intrigued him with their sterility and cold. "I sense many hands in its creation. It's now a beast thirsty for more souls."

He swept through the morgue. Fenix heard the ambulances reversing in the unloading bay. More bodies were coming in.

"And my dear, Kemeticism is just a word. A term. To describe something luminous. Do not be fooled by pretty words," he muttered.

"Lord, what are my… instructions?" Fenix raised her head, realizing that she kept it bowed for the entire duration.

Yinepu was already gone, like a dream.

***

"You found a Singaporean *Chinese* embalmer to do your bidding?!" Sekhmet's voice was incredulous. Indeed, she stood arms akimbo on her hips. Unfettered by human guises, she now blazed with the sun's power.

Yinepu glanced at her mildly, also in his jackal form. He twirled his sceptre contemplatively. "She's one who listens. And my dear sister, she's not 'doing my bidding'".

"We are Netjeru. Powers." When Sekhmet calmed down, the sun went behind a cloud. Yinepu was secretly relieved that at least, the halls of Maat weren't bathed in blinding light. Souls travelling this way to have their hearts weighted shouldn't be terrified even more by Sekhmet's solar light. Sekhmet was simply Sekhmet, all glorious sun, fire and rage.

The sceptre tapped empty air once, twice. "Even Powers are subject to outside Powers. This Darkness is out of our control."

"I will go question Set. He has too much time on his hands."

"What will it accomplish, my dear sister? Shake his head like a calabash and hope something falls out?"

"If there's something there in the first place," Sekhmet growled and the sun glimmered in her form. Yinepu much wished that calmer and kinder Bast was in her place instead. Bast had been running around too, kept busy by requests from frightened petitioners. The Darkness was scaring them. He was sure that Sekhmet had heard cries from her followers too.

"We can also seek our shemsu for help," he suggested.

"They are running like spineless fools."

"They are running like spineless fools because they are scared."

"How can you be so calm, brother?" A shake of her mane indicated her disbelief.

Yinepu shrugged. "What else can we do?"

"Rip the Darkness into shreds, blast it into nothing?" Sekhmet pointed a clawed finger at him. She was after all Netjeru of war and healing. *Also war and rage and pestilence*, Yinepu amended to himself.

"Oh, my lioness warrior sister," Yinepu shook his head too. "Our father Ra will be upset with you. What will your consort Ptah say? That Sekhmet has gone rampaging again?"

"And placate me with blood wine later to get me too drunk to care? Your tongue is bladed today, brother."

"I am just concerned. As I have said, the Darkness is beyond our control. Set, or people beyond Set's domain... have created it. Ah, ah, ah, still your tongue – we are not going after the creators. Yet."

"I hope," Sekhmet exhaled out slowly, letting out her banked rage. It was said that her breath formed the sands of Egypt. "I hope your embalmer is indeed the right choice."

Yinepu tilted his head and rested his chin on his sceptre. "I hope so too."

***

Fenix lit a candle before the small statue of Yinepu. Popular culture called him Anubis. But she often felt that Yinepu was a truer and deeper name for the jackal-headed god of the dead. She offered him a small porcelain tea cup filled with pineapple beer. It was the only thing she could find in the fridge. Her father liked pineapple beer, his current craze for the moment.

"Pineapple beer," a male voice, smooth like the best of butter, flowed into the room and around her. "Ah, delectable."

She didn't look up. She already knew that it was Yinepu.

"Beer was first created in my land," Yinepu sniffed the beer appreciatively. "People were quick to mix grains with water. Now, we have pineapple beer. Taiwan, isn't it?"

"You know it's from Taiwan, lord?" Fenix looked up then, and saw his amber eyes. He was in his black suit and pants, but his jackal head shone through. His human form was handsome – dark haired, brown skin. He looked like one of those Hollywood leading men with Arabic features.

"I have shemsu and followers in Taiwan," he toasted her.

"Oh," Fenix felt like a little girl being told off and tried to sit up straighter, more adult. "Oh, what are my instructions?"

"Ah," Yinepu downed the beer. It was sweet, with a strong hint of malt, wheat and pineapple. "Come with me."

"Where?" Fenix blinked.

"To Duat. Land of the dead."

She didn't feel him grab her hand. The transition from land of the living to land of the dead was too quick, like a dizzy spin.

Hot air blasted into her face. Hot desert air, reminding her of the time she travelled to Perth, Western Australia, and it was the peak of summer. Hot, dry, sand-dry. She recovered enough to see a parched land, like all the deserts in her Secondary Four Geography textbook combined, with a crimson, blood-red sky. *Typical*, the snide calm voice of rationality said in her head. *Typical. Desert people.*

Yet the entire place beggared belief. She was never a desert person. Had never been to a desert, except the Sand Dunes of Perth, but they were never a true desert. Singapore doesn't have deserts. It is tropical. It has monsoons. It is always and constantly humid. This place was awe-inspiring and terrifying: it was devoid of life. Nothing. Except for the pulsing red sky.

There were spots of darkness, miniature nights captured and growing by the minute. They moved in a desultory manner. Like a horde. Like refugees running away from wars. Weary. Fatigue beyond fatigue. Death walking. She heard a crying and chilled her blood. It was both sobbing and weeping.

"Our people are dying," Yinepu's voice came from her right. She tried to orientate herself. The place confused her. The sand stretched out everywhere. There were no landmarks. Nothing. No trees. No rocks. Nothing. "Those are souls evicted from their bodies far too early by the Darkness."

"You mean the virus."

"Darkness. Virus. It's still the same. People die because of it."

Fenix finally fixed her attention on Yinepu, now in his full jackal-head god form. He was imposing, just as she thought he would be. A sadness, however, tinged his figure. His mighty shoulders sagged, as if wearied, burdened.

"Do you want me to find…a cure?" Fenix asked.

"No," Yinepu said firmly. "I do not want heroics. I want you… to remind me that I am Netjeru, that as Powers, we could beat the Darkness back into the void it came from. I want you to believe in me. "

Fenix's knees were jelly. She sank onto the sand. It was warm, surprisingly comforting, and so very fine.

"That stunned you, my child?" Yinepu's voice was amused, kind.

"Yes. I always thought that gods do not need to be reminded of their existence."

"Oh, that's sheer hubris, this arrogance that we are above all. We exist, because of you. You exist, because of us. Simple as that. There is a relationship, an exchange of energy. A symbiosis, if you want to use fancy words. Oh, damn…"

Fenix heard the alarm in his voice, wasn't surprised that he swore.

The dark spots were coalescing.

***

Elsewhere, the news agencies were afire with panic, fed by the larger panic of the governments trying to stop the deaths from increasing. The apocalypse was becoming real too quickly.

Somewhere, a Darkness roared and laughed and roared.

***

"Consider the body," Yinepu was still speaking as he ran up the sand dune easily, his sceptre now a blazing spear, his other hand holding a silver khopesh as long as Fenix was tall. Fenix lagged behind, cursing at the curling sand beneath her feet. "Consider the body and its myriad functions. The skull, beautifully formed, houses the brains which control the rest of the body – limbs, hands, organs. Each blood vessel is like a river. Imagine the Nile, flowing, fed by its tributaries. Each is important. Each is interdependent."

"A symbiosis," Fenix supplied, inclining her head in agreement. She was surprised to see that she was now wearing brown leather armor. It covered her torso, while giving her enough mobility. She felt secure. Oh yes, she held a khopesh too and the balance was right in her hand. The curved weapon gleamed with its own light.

Yinepu smiled. "Good, my child, you are getting my point." He crested the top of the dune and stood there, his ears swivelled forward as if listening for a particular sound. In the unlight of the Duat, his dark fur rippled with bronze highlights.

"Go for the head?" Fenix concluded. "Or the heart?"

"You are an embalmer. You are intimate with the functions of the body. All of my priests are. And, if I could recall, you are also a trained doctor, are you not?"

Fenix stopped in her track, the sand hissing softly at her feet. She noticed she was now wearing boots. They felt soft, like treated goat's skin. Lovingly tanned and stretched. "Yes, I am."

All the years of studying in the local university's medical school down the drain, her father would complain to her, even though he was pleased that she wanted to be part of his business, Lee Huat Funeral Services. She did that prerequisite one year of housemanship at one of the major government hospitals, found it too unpalatable, and quit after that. She couldn't even be a general practitioner. Nevertheless, she studied embalming and obtained her license. Her job, however, got her few friends. The ones she had still thought she was weird or morbid or both. She spent her weekends photographing wildlife. Solitary life seemed so much better.

"How would you treat a sick man?" Yinepu knelt down, sniffing the air. "You look for symptoms."

"My lord, you want me to look for the head of... Darkness?"

"*Us.* We are going for it," Yinepu smiled again. "Both head and heart, if you will. Ah, I believe that is my sister."

A walking sun approached them from Fenix's right. She shook from top to bottom. That was Sekhmet. Lion-headed, solar disk on her head, and flaming khopesh in her claw. On her back slung a quiver of arrows.

"Ah, well-met, brother," the lion-headed woman bowed slightly. "And to you, mortal."

Fenix was so stunned she couldn't speak.

"Brother, is your follower both deaf and mute?" A feral smile curled Sekhmet's lips. It took a while for Fenix to realize that it was a friendly smile.

"She's just stunned by your glorious light," Yinepu shrugged nonchalantly and continued his survey of the land and the growing mass of darkness in front of them.

"My lady Sekhmet," Fenix found her voice, remembered the words she read once on a website dedicated to Sekhmet. "Glorious and honored are you, great warrioress."

"She has a voice and a silver tongue," Sekhmet said drily, but with humor.

"Fenix," Yinepu drew attention to himself, beckoning to her. It was incongruous: she standing in the middle of two giant animal-headed beings in Egyptian headdress and garb. "Fenix, it's time to use your skills."

"I don't have any skills."

"Nonsense, my child," Yinepu's amber eyes flared up and this time, she could feel his frustration. "You deny it all the time, using *science* as an excuse."

Her professors and doctor-clinicians would often berate her for using intuition. She often *knew* why the patient was sick or where the pain was coming from. She just did. *You are a medical doctor*, they scolded her. *Use your medical knowledge.* If she continued as a general practitioner, she would have incorporated traditional Chinese medicine. The body meridians were as clear to her as day. They pulsed, clean of debris, if the patient was fine. They were murky or clogged, if there was an issue. She recalled Yinepu's description of the body vessels as rivers.

"Focus on that *thing*," revulsion filled Yinepu's normally calm voice. "It looks like it's mutating, growing arms and more arms."

Fenix stared at the Darkness, knowing that in the land of the living, it was the terrifying virus killing thousands, perhaps even millions. *Do gods get old? Do they die? Are they supposed to be eternal?* With a shudder that was part fear, part elation, she concentrated on the Darkness, imagining that it had a body, that it had a nervous system, that it had a heart (or hearts). Most of all, she imagined that it had a head that coordinated the virus.

Suddenly, she was *inside* the Darkness, inside its throbbing cell that served as its heart and brain and soul. She was floating in it, yet there was no liquid. For a moment, she panicked and flailed. The t-shaped cells flowing about her darted frantically.

Get a grip, Fenix thought sternly and forced herself to hang motionless. It was an American aphorism. She tried to think like her mother. *Man man lai*. Let's slow down. Let's not worry too much. She exhaled and her head slowly cleared. *Think*, she thought furiously, *think*.

She blinked, once, twice. There, nestled in the middle of sinews, was the nucleus. The heart and brain. It gleamed at her like an evil orange eye straight from a fantasy movie.

"Right there! Right there, lord!" Fenix found herself shouting.

Then she was right out of the Darkness, back where she was, standing with the Netjeru. She swayed on her feet, dizzy.

"Indeed, you have found the heart," Yinepu's grin was totally jackal now. "Sekhmet? Are you ready?"

Sekhmet saluted with her khopesh. "Can you not feel my battle joy, brother?"

"I trust that other Netjeru and Powers from other traditions are ready too. Have you sent them word?"

Of course Yinepu was not a violent individual per se and he often opposed direct confrontation. Some things you just cannot fight. Yet, the Darkness wasn't something to ignore. People were dying by the thousands. He had no choice, but to send out a Call. He even asked his father. The situation was that desperate

Sekhmet smiled wider, baring her fangs. She lifted her maned head and roared. It was a roar worthy of a prehistoric carnosaur. Fenix squeezed her eyes shut at the sheer power. It was both sound and physical force. Voices answered. Resonant, powerful voices that pierced through her bones. They came around all directions. A fierce joy rushed through her. She shouted too, shaking her khopesh, as if she was a warrior.

***

Hospitals were filled to their full capacity when the Darkness reached its peak during its killing spree, indulging its blood thirst. Yet at the worst, when the streets of every major city were empty of pedestrians and traffic, when the wail of ambulances and police cars was the only music to adults and children, something happened. The Darkness started to recede.

Some commentators said that they had found a vaccine, at a horrible cost. Doctors and researchers sacrificed their lives to find the cure to an apparently incurable disease. There were people who were more cynical and suggested that the Darkness had reached its natural limit and like tides, had begun ebbing away.

As it were, people started to recover.

Those who sat up abruptly on their hospital beds, startling the ICU nurses, told of a bright star centering in their chests and the noise of a war in their heads. When the star burst, they felt as if they were made whole. They couldn't explain it, only to say that the star chased the darkness away.

The war continued.

***

Fenix was in a middle of a war.

She was the only privileged individual to witness such a war conducted on such a scale. She was the only mortal watching Powers and gods and goddess wage war with Darkness.

She saw gods from every tradition, every culture, appear in the land of the dead, each ablaze with his or her or its own light, bearing the weapons and tools of their own particular faith. They came in different forms and sizes and shapes: human, non-human, animal, not of Earth origin. She swore she saw Shiva, the Destroyer, shredding pieces of the Darkness, burning them into embers. Durga rode her tiger into battle, with Sekhmet beside her, roaring their own battle cries. She saw Ra, Horus, Sobek and Hathor, their light overwhelming and searingly bright to her eyes. She saw the Norse gods and goddesses too, Odin and Frigga leading the charge. Thor shouted and thunder boomed overhead. Gods and goddesses unleashed whatever they had, sending beams of light or fire or power into the Darkness. Closer to home were gods and goddesses from her Taoist faith. With a ferocious visage, Kuan Kong stormed in and slashed the

Darkness with his jian and enormous halberd. Even the Monkey God twirled his pole and beat the tendrils of the Darkness, hooting joyously.

Bit by bit, part by part, they were gaining ground. Darkness receded, backing away into a corner. It snarled now, a mass of bristling black hair, looking for in the world like an offended cat with bottle-brush tail and hissing bravado.

Someone howled, a long ululation of tortured agony – and it was a little orange spider, scuttling out of the black hair.

Ra smashed it to the ground, pulped it and made sure it didn't run away. It reminded Fenix, somewhat, of the very-dead mud crabs her dad liked to cook for special occasions: all exposed guts and broken chitin and limbs.

"And one more," she heard Yinepu say to the horde of gods and goddesses. He reached into the mass of black hair and extracted a glowing sickly stone. It pulsed a dull orange-amber.

"Ah, Set, ah, Apophis, ah the dark Powers, now we deal with thee," he intoned and clearly that was a ritual, a challenge to unseen foes and enemies. With a snarl, he crushed it in his fist.

A long scream trailed in the distance, abruptly, suddenly choked off. To Fenix, it sounded angry, rage-filled, and so, so very thwarted.

"Finally," Ra, his form glimmering with inner light, like a banked sun. "Done. This was indeed a good way to entice me out of my retirement."

Yinepu bowed low, acknowledging the compliment.

"People still believe in us," the Goddess Kuan Yin, in robes the color of the white full moon, said. Her voice was gentle, compassionate. "Now let the healing begin." She tipped the small vase she was carrying. Clear water trickled out, plopping into the fine sand of Duat. The sand drank it in. Heart-shaped sorrel emerged forth, carpeting the desert.

"They do," Fenix said. "We still do."

With wonder, she knelt down and touched the heart-shaped sorrel.

***

When she returned back to the land of the living, the candle had burned low. Time had obviously passed. Yet she looked at the alarm clock beside her bed, it was 6 in the morning. Her entire body ached. She had abrasions along her legs and thighs. Sand could be quite unkind.

She was still holding her khopesh. In the land of the living, it had shrunk to the size of a dagger. A laugh welled up from inside her. What would her father say this time?

Still laughing, she placed the khopesh before the statue of Yinepu, slipped out of her t-shirt and shorts, and prepared for a new day at the morgue.

***

The Darkness, as people had called it, simply stopped infecting. The news agencies called it a 'miracle'. Apocalypse averted, they said in breathless tones. Now people, let's concentrate on healing and re-building what we have lost. The news now was replete with donation drives and testimonies from people who had recovered miraculously. People were eager to get Darkness behind them.

Belief in the Divine, in whatever form, found a new resurgence. Devotees thronged shrines and temples.

Somewhere, Yinepu smiled and enjoyed a glass of wine.

Exant

Crystal Sarakas

The air was thick with smoke and ash, riding the breeze that kept the fires going. He climbed the last few feet to the top of the ridge and stood there, breathing in the acrid stench of gas and wood and hair and skin. He stood there, the nearly full moon lighting up the scrub desert around him, and looked down upon the city below. Only a few weeks ago, its artificial lights had lit up the desert, the sounds of a million people fighting and rutting and dreaming spreading out over the earth's skin. Now, the city burned, all the cities burned, and the fighting and rutting and dreaming had turned to screaming and crying and praying as the humans found themselves being ushered out the door of existence.

It was glorious and heartbreaking all at the same time.

He knew when she arrived, the wind swirling around him, heralding her presence. His nostrils flared, taking in her scent. It had been a long time since he had last seen her, a time measured not in years but eons. Too long spent alone, wandering the world, always looking but never touching.

"Luciver." She walked up to him, her arms sliding up his in greeting. He leaned into her, his forehead pressed against hers, inhaling deeply. His wings swept forward around her, the light from the fires below shimmering along his feathers.

"Muriel." His voice was deep, raspy with disuse. He held her close, content to simply breathe in the sweet spiciness of her scent, to twine his fingers in her long, auburn hair.

She turned in his arms to look out over the burning city. "It's hard to believe they are finally going to be gone," she said. "After all these millions of years, it ends with us."

"Shall we go down and watch?" he asked, fingers entwining with hers.

"Yes."

***

They walked along a street, hand in hand. Trash littered the street, all the things that humans thought worth saving. He stopped by one open suitcase, a glimmer of gold winking in the firelight. He pulled a necklace from the case, admiring it as it poured like molten flame through his fingers. "Here," he said, holding it out to her. "A present."

She smiled, delighted. "So pretty!"

Something groaned nearby. The turned their heads, eyes searching the darkness. "Just one," he said, watching the shambling ruins of a man lumbering toward them. Luciver walked up to him, hands gently reaching out to cup the man's face, staring into his ruined eyes, before crushing his skull in.

"One less," she replied.

***

They wandered for weeks, sometimes taking one of the cars that had been scattered across the roadways like marbles and driving to a new city to see the same destruction. Sometimes they flew, losing themselves in the thermals that were free of the stench of death. Neither of them talked much, having run out of things to say. Luciver glanced behind him from time to time, wondering if one of the Others would show up to enforce the decree that none of the fallen were to congregate. But the skies were silent, empty. He wondered if Michael and the others were dead too.

"What do you think did it?" Muriel asked one night as they sat on top of a building. She gestured at the ruins below. "What caused all this?"

"Some kind of plague. If it had been war, there might be have some normal humans left, but those things we keep finding are just … shells. Mindless creatures."

"Do you think there are humans left alive?"

"Probably. Somewhere. But I doubt they will matter much in the end. Too scattered, too used to living in comfort. They won't survive without help." He knew that this time there would be no divine nudge to keep humanity going. Heaven's landlord had been missing since the Fall, and even the loyal no longer believed he would return.

After a long while, she stirred. "What will happen to us when they are all dead?"

Luciver turned to look at her, his eyes shadowed. "I don't know."

***

They stood in the center of a church, watching the rising sun pour its rays through the stained glass windows, colors shimmering across the pews and bodies lying there.

"So many came here to die," she said, walking along the aisle, her fingers smoothing the hair back from one woman's face, or stopping to cup a child's face. "Why here?" she asked, turning to look at him. "Don't they know that He died long ago?"

"This is where they believed," he said. "They thought that a god loved them, would die for them, would save them. So they came here when all hope had gone, believing that this would be the one place to hold back death."

"How primitive," she mused, "for a species that grew so powerful, so dangerous, to believe in such a thing."

"Don't forget that it was us who taught them." He was quiet for a long moment. "I think, in the end, it's part of why they died. They relied on promises that would be fulfilled beyond death, and so they ignored what was right here. Not all of them," he said, "but enough to doom them."

Muriel narrowed her eyes. "You sound as if you mourn them."

"Perhaps, just a little. They were so full of hate and senseless violence, but so much beauty too, for creatures that lived only a handful of decades. What have we done that has left such a mark on the world?"

Muriel raised an eyebrow. "I had no idea you liked them so much."

Luciver didn't answer. They wound through the pews and up the stairs of the altar, staring up at the man hanging on the cross. Not the carved wood version; someone had apparently decided that these times demanded a real sacrifice, and had offered up one of their priests here. He hung there, naked, except for the cross he wore around his neck. Rust-red pools of blood stained the altar below him.

Muriel gestured. "Did they think sacrificing another son would bring him back?"

"No." He stared at the hanging man. "This was desperation, nothing more."

"Well, hey there. I thought I sensed someone else in the neighborhood."

Luciver whirled. He knew that voice, even if he hadn't heard it in ages. "Samael," he growled. "What are you doing on this side of the ocean?"

"Same as you, brother. Celebrating the end of the apes, maybe looking for a party." He winked at Muriel. "Or maybe for a fight. Nice to see you, darlin'. It's been too long."

Muriel eyed him as she sniffed the air. "You're not alone," she said.

"No, he's not." Another woman stepped out of the shadows, her eyes a bright emerald green. She walked over to Samael, linking her arm through his. "Muriel. You're looking positively cadaverous. Haven't you been feeding? I mean, there's plenty of unspoiled meat still walking around."

"You know that Luciver doesn't like us feeding on the humans, Sibyl. No path to redemption there," Muriel said, a hint of nastiness in her voice.

"Well," Samael said, scratching his head as he looked around the church. "I don't exactly see much chance of redemption anymore, what with all the death and destruction going on. Come on, brother. I can tell you haven't truly fed in ages."

"They're perfectly ripe," Sibyl added. "So much fear, so much despair. Like the finest wine sliding down your throat."

Luciver grabbed Muriel by the arm. "We don't feed on the humans," he said, his words clipped, 'so if you will excuse us..."

"What's the rush?" Samael moved to block the doorway, his inky black wings spread wide. "Haven't seen you in ages, and you want to rush off without even a how-do?"

Luciver rubbed his eyes, a bone-deep weariness settling over him. "I don't know about you, but I don't relish a fight with the guardians," he said. "It's risky enough to be paired up with Muriel, but all of us together are going to get their attention."

Samael rolled his eyes. "Oh, whatever, dude. Michael! Gabriel!" he shouted, head thrown back to the sky. "Hey! A bunch of fallen down here about to have a party! Better come kick our asses! We might get all rowdy and uppity again! Might even bring about the end of the world with our shenanigans! Oh wait," he said, sneering. "The world done gone up and ended itself."

Luciver slammed Samael into the wall, his forearm tight against the other angel's throat. "I do not wish to get their attention," he snarled into Samael's slowly purpling face. "I am going to leave, you are not going to follow, and that is going to be the end of it. Agreed?" At Samael's nod, he stepped back, then lashed out without warning, his fist slamming into Samael's face. He started to walk out the door as Samael crumpled to the ground, then stopped, growling as Sibyl made a move as if to block him.

"Sibyl. Leave it be." Luciver stood still, his shadow looming behind him on the church wall.

Samael had picked himself up off the floor, his blood a bright-red smear across his mouth. "Don't worry, love," he spat. "That was just a lovetap. Let's go, Sibyl. He's still caught up in the same guilt-trip that sent him down the rabbit hole two-thousand years ago. No fun to be had here."

Luciver heard it first, a tiny mewling sound coming from one of the pews. Before he could move, Samael had crossed the room, shoving the bloated body of a woman off one of the pews. "Woowee! Here's a little ape all wrapped up like a candy cane at Christmas!" He held up a squirming red and white bundle, the blanket carefully wrapped around a small child. Luciver had no idea how the baby was still alive.

"Samael. Give the child to me." Luciver spoke softly, his eyes intent on the pitifully small bundle in Samael's arms.

Samael looked at Luciver, that cocksure grin back on his face. "Oh? Want to eat him yourself?"

Luciver held himself motionless, fighting the need, the desire so sharp it made his chest hurt, to save that tiny little human. But he just stood there, watching as Samael snapped the tiny little human's tiny little neck. "Muriel. We're leaving."

He didn't walk away fast enough to not hear the sound of Samael feeding.

***

Luciver stalked through the streets, his hands clenched into fists inside his pockets, Muriel trailing after him. He could feel the weight of her stare against his shoulder blades. Her judgment. "You have something to say?" he snarled over his shoulder, slowing so she could step up beside him.

"Only that you seem to have forgotten what it means to be us, Luciver. You are no longer the morning star. You are a demon. A devil. THE devil. You led us all into hell and yet you stand here, lording above us, too good to feed or revel in the chaos around us."

Luciver stopped and turned. "Don't you understand? Have you seriously never regretted what we did that day? We were wrong, Muriel! We had no right to fight, to rebel against our father. And instead of admitting it, of throwing ourselves at his mercy and begging to go back home, I had to go and fuck up his pride and joy." He grabbed her arms and whirled her around. "Look, Muriel! Look at the corpses, the bloat, the dead children lying in their mothers arms. I did this! I did it!"

Muriel elbowed him hard in the ribs and spun around to face him. "You whiny little child! You arrogant prick! You didn't cause the end of the world. It was a damn plague, remember? The humans did it to themselves! You're not mighty enough, not important enough to have that much power anymore! You're a pathetic shadow of the creature I loved." She spit in his face. "You're no better than those mewling apes."

He let her go, sinking slowly to his knees. He didn't cry. Tears were a luxury he had spent long ago. Now, he was small, hunched. He looked up at Muriel, flinching back from the scorn in her eyes. "You're going to die, Muriel. I'm going to die. We don't exist in a world without him, without humans. And you don't even know it yet." He wiped his dry eyes with the back of his hand and heaved to his feet. "Are you going to leave me now?" he asked. He looked up when there was no answer. She was gone.

***

He had traveled the Midwest in solitude of a sort, slinking through cities gone mad in the final death throes of civilization. More often, he had to take to the skies to stay out of reach of the shambling ruins that now hunted anything that moved, driven by some primal urge to mimic life. He never felt alone, though. He knew Muriel was out there, pacing him but staying out of sight.

The sun was high in the sky, the stink of rotting flesh starting to fade as flesh was stripped from bone by feeders, insects, and worms. The natural world was slowly rebooting itself, sloughing off the trauma of the last few months like a snake shedding her skin. He was flying, low enough to be able to peer into the windows of some of the taller buildings. He was searching, his aimless wandering slowly being consumed by a drive to find some sign, any sign, that the end of the world wasn't actually here, no matter what horrors cried their truth all around him.

He heard the screams first, bouncing off brick and glass like doppler echoes. He pumped his wings as he gained height, scanning the ground below. Those screams didn't sound like the feeders, they sounded alive. He spotted them, a small band of people huddled together in a defensive arc. They had chosen their ground well, set inside a gated courtyard that had once housed the wealthy and elderly. The building curved out at their backs, a sentinel offering as much passive shelter as possible.

He hovered over the group. He may not be able to save the rest of the world, but he could handle one group of feeders. A truck had crashed on the street, its nose coming to rest against the iron bars separating the courtyard from the rest of the world. A handful of feeders had figured out how to climb, and were shambling over the nose of the truck and across the fence. He landed near the first one, striding up behind it and snapping its neck before it could turn to face him. He crushed the skull of the second one in with one hand, feeling the bones crumble like pebbles inside the ruined skin that still clung to the skeleton. The third fell easily, but he found himself on his back, barely holding off the last one that had managed to trip him. This was one was still strong and relatively fresh. Luciver strained to keep its teeth from biting into his neck, and frantically looked around for some kind of weapon.

There was a meaty crack, and a spray of blackened blood and bone spattered his face. The corpse fell to the ground, looking surprised. Luciver looked up into Muriel's face, at the axe she held in her hands. 'Thank you," he said, rolling to his side and spitting out gobs of the creature's brains.

"Don't mention it." Muriel crossed over to stand in front of the small band of humans still pressed against the stone wall. "I can't believe you actually found a group of live ones." She turned to look back at Luciver, her face and teeth elongating. "Come. Feed with me. Regain your strength." She held out her hand, her fingers scaly and ridged with scars, her nails lengthened into daggers.

Luciver stared at her, then looked at the humans. They were a pathetic group. Five adults, three children, all of them dirty and gaunt, clearly starving. They stared back at the two angels, hope and fear warring on their faces. Why not feed? What was the point of his self-imposed rules? He felt his own teeth shift, and the hunger that he had ignored for so long roared through him, a serpent coiling to strike. He took one step, then another.

One of the children pointed at him. "Mommy! An angel! Maybe he'll take us up to heaven to be with Grammy and PopPop!"

Luciver snarled. Muriel had slipped up beside him, her features no longer the quiet beauty of his dreams and heart. She was fully demon now, and intent only on the prey standing before. Together, they paced forward, wings spread, hunting even when their target couldn't run.

One of the human males screamed as he pointed a shotgun at Muriel. Luciver closed the distance between them in a heartbeat, wrenching the weapon away with his right hand. His left hand closed around the human's throat and he turned to Muriel. "Do you want him?"

"Yes," she hissed, her forked tongue flicking out to lick her lips. "Bleed him for me. I want to taste it on my tongue."

Something flickered in Luciver's eyes, some remnant of memory long suppressed. "Come darling. We'll drink him dry together."

Luciver twisted the man's head to the side, his eyes locked on Muriel's. He bit once, striking the neck and tearing a gash. Crimson flowed down the dirt and sweat stained neck, the odor of urine rising from where the human pissed himself. Muriel inhaled, her eyes closed, her face an unholy rictus of pleasure as she leaned forward to feed.

That was when Luciver thrust the shotgun into her chest, the cold steel shattering her ribcage, and pulled the trigger.

***

He had made it all the way to the ocean, looking out across the Atlantic, the towering sentinels of New York lost somewhere behind him. This, at least, looked the way it always had, a great, vast heaving of grey and white foam, lapping at the sand under his feet.

He walked around the city, the strike of his footsteps swallowed by the looming silence around him. In that tiny building, he had once stood for hours, staring at a single painting by some unknown - and now dead - artist. He had sat through countless films, lost in the celluloid dreams of another for hour after hour. He stood before the great twin lions of the library, their marble bodies blackened by ash from the burning books that fell softly around them, like snow.

"Still here, brother?" Samael's voice was ragged, tasting of acrid meat and rot. He spat, a great gob of red-tinged mucus. "Still moping about the apes?"

Luciver turned to look at him. Samael's eyes were sunken in, their glow dimmed now. His skin was ashen, his wings trailed limply behind him, pinions writing gibberish in the dirt. He neck and shoulder were covered in festering bites. "You're sick," Luciver said. "You let them feed on you."

Samael shrugged. The gesture threw him off-balance and he half-fell, half-sat on the ground, his wings crushed beneath him. "Fuck me," he laughed. "Got caught by one while enjoying another. They were tasty, but damn if they aren't going to kill me in the end."

Luciver knelt before him, gripping Samael's head in his hands. "Where is Sibyl, Samael? Where is your sister?"

Samael didn't answer. He just stared, his eyes slipping past Luciver to focus on some point, some image, seen only by his fevered brain.

Lucivar gathered Samael's body in his arms, and launched himself skyward. Samael had been a coward, his long existence full of atrocity and the horrors he rained down upon his victims, but still, Luciver couldn't leave him there to rot, or worse, to become one of the walking shells. He flew for hours, watching as the concrete buildings beneath him gave way to forest and rivers. He spiraled down, his eyes on a shimmering lake surrounded hemmed in by a vast expanse of green. No humans had settled here, at least not in any great numbers.

He landed, gently lowering the body to the ground. The lake would suit his purpose. He might even linger here, away from the cities of the dead. He spent the afternoon gathering branches from the surrounding woods, weaving them together with vines he pulled from where they grew along the dirt road that ran through the forest.

He moved Samael's body to the raft, watching as it settled deeper into the water before lifting up again, finding its balance. He tried to speak, to say something before he sent the corpse off into the lake, but nothing came. No words of comfort, no fond memories. He shrugged and then bent down to push the raft toward the lake, walking until the water rose mid-thigh before he gave it one final shove and let it go.

The sinking sun turned the surface of the water into fire, swallowing the shadow of the raft and its burden. Luciver gestured once, and real flames billowed up to meet celestial fire. He watched, ignoring the buzzing of insects flitting through each exhaled breath until the fire sank into nothing, taking the charred remains of what was once an angel of God with it.

He spend the night there on the bank of the lake, lying on his back, wings spread out over the grass. The stars were bright here, fiercer with the absence of moon or sun. The dark wasn't quiet though; the whir of a thousand insects, the high-pitched chitter of the bats that hunted them, even the cracking twigs and snorts as a herd of deer wandered by him to drink their fill at the water's edge. It was noisier here than the last cities he had been in. There was life here, blazing forth in all its faunic glory.

He was still awake when the sun came. He watched as the shadows retreated around him, felt the first warmth of day as the rays stole over the treetops, filling the meadow with light. He had just about decided to never move from this spot again when he heard it. A laugh. A child's laugh.

He was on his feet before his brain told him to stand. His head turned, listening, trying to locate the laughter. Was he going mad? Was this how his days would end? Haunted by the spirits of those he had walked away from?

He heard it again, the silvery peal of laughter that was answered by another voice. He ran, pushing against tree limbs and brambles, heedless of the lashes and cuts that stung his skin, ignoring the pain as feathers were torn from his wings.

He stumbled out into a clearing. The trees seemed to recede around him, framing the valley he stood in. Rows of corn and sunflowers edged a field, heads dancing in the early breeze. He could see a vegetable garden near a house, well-tended. The house itself was small, but tidy, its clapboards freshly painted and gleaming white and gold in the sunlight. He heard the laughter again and watched, heart in his throat, as two small figures tumbled from the doorway to the house, dancing around each other.

"So innocent. It reminds me of another time long ago."

Luciver closed his eyes, unwilling to see who he knew was standing next to him. "Why?" he asked. "Why show me this? Why, when they're going to die too?"

"Are they?" The voice sounded surprised. "I didn't know that. It's not in my plan."

"How are two small children going to survive in this world for long? In case you missed the signs, the world is ended. Gone. The horsemen rode. Hail the Apocalypse." Luciver felt the bitterness tumble over his lips, tasting of bile and tears. "You left us!" he shouted. "We were just children, we didn't know any better, and you just walked away! And look at us! Look at what we did to the world! We ruined everything!"

The tears came then, unleashed, great wracking sobs that hammered him to his knees. "I'm so sorry, I'm so sorry," he gasped, the words falling out of his mouth in a torrent of pain and regret. "We ruined everything. I ruined everything."

"Oh my child." The voice changed, shifting from the dark baritone of his father, to the gentle alto of his mother. "So much despair, so much darkness. We are so sorry for what you endured, we grieved for you, but you left us no choice."

Luciver lay there, his head resting on the knees of his Creator. The tears slowed, leaving behind furrows in the dirt and grime etched into his face. A hand smoothed gently over his hair, fingers working the tangles loose, brushing over his head over and over again. The same hands washed his face, wiping away the last trace of tears and sorrow.

"Will you let them die, Morningstar?" His father again. "Or will you watch over them, protect them as they grow to maturity, to be the mother and father of a new age?"

Luciver looked up, at the shining face that slipped between mother and father and back again. "They... is there really a chance?" He held his breath, the whole world held its breath, waiting for the answer.

"Brother, there is always a chance." Samael smiled at him, his face whole and happy, the face of the angel he had been before the Fall.

Luciver turned back to the children, who now stood, hand in hand, watching them. He took a few steps toward them, then looked back at the empty meadow.

"Thank you," he said to no one. He walked over to where the children stood, staring at him. Their faces were clean, washed, their cheeks chubby and bellies rounded. They were loved, protected here in this garden.

"Hello," the young girl said. "My name is Amara. This is Malik. This is our home. Are you going to live with us now?" She stared at him, her gaze solemn, weighing him against some invisible scale.

"Will you be our father? We haven't had one up until now."

Luciver stared at them, his heart pounding in his ears. "I think so," he said, holding out his hands. They each grabbed one, pulling him toward the doorway.

"Come inside!" Amara said. "We're hungry! Can you cook breakfast?"

Luciver laughed. "I can certainly try. What do you want?"

Malik thought for a long moment, his face serious. "I want pancakes and ice cream. And maybe some kale."

"Ew! Kale is gross." The two children scampered across the room to the kitchen table, arguing over which food in the entire world was the grossest and nastiest and pukiest. Luciver crossed into the kitchen, then froze when he spied the bowl on the counter. Apples, red and glistening, were piled in a bowl, leaves and branches carved onto the ceramic surface.

The children were suddenly quiet, staring at him with eyes far older than their years. "Don't worry, Luciver," Malik said, his lips curling up in a smile. "My sister really doesn't like apples. She thinks they are completely gross."

Ice and Fire

M. J. King

The end of the world is here, and it has come in fire and ice. I would like it to hurry up. Some gain patience with long years, but I am not one of them.

The two armies thunder and crash in the valley below. Steam geysers through the sulfurous smog. Sometimes I catch a glimpse of them through the eddies of yellow-green mist: a glint off a carapace of ice so pure as to be nearly clear, or the dark-burning embers of their opposition. Today, I follow the battle through sound alone.

The fire giants roar as they break through. Ice gives a creaky bellow in desperate reply, their forces scattering further, as I'd promised fire. More steam plumes high in the thin, thin atmosphere.

And I stand on the crystal slope of a mountain, far above the carnage, as I imagine any god still living must watch over us all. That comes as small comfort; only the trickster gods must be left now.

"Here you are."

I turn to see Kyalikkeh gliding toward me, six legs scrabbling on slick crystal, foreclaws waving in agitation. I tap out a welcome that hangs in the air like a chorus of bells. The world has made herself our instrument, and we've learned to make music with her. I think it is her apology that even she must end.

"Did you expect me to be anywhere else?"

She doesn't answer, just rotates her eyestalks to the roiling, noxious fog below and says, "You can't even see them today."

"Ah, but I see it all in my mind."

"Her head waves side to side in exasperation. "That makes even less sense."

I flap a claw at her. "It's my entertainment. I don't need you to understand."

But she settles beside me, gaze intent on the earth below, as though she can part the smog by sheer willpower. "Are you really so bored? We're all struggling here, Talitikke, but we are trying to make something of a life. Why must you play with fire?"

"And ice," I saw. "Don't forget them — slights live on in their racial memories."

The blow from her claw rocks me. The fan of my tail scrapes a discordant chime from the ground, but I keep my balance. Barely.

Perhaps I deserved that.

"Have you always been like this?" She demands. "So cynical. You must have been different once, before me."

There is no 'before' her worth remembering, but I don't tell her that. Once of us with an overinflated sense of self importance is enough.

"You should stop playing these games. What if they figure you out?"

"They won't." This is an old argument. Then again, is there any other kind, at the end of everything? "They're not that smart."

Again, her head waves side to side. "Hubris, Talittikke, hubris."

"If only they would prove me wrong. I would rejoice in the unpredictability."

"Enough to keep you from the Walk?"

Is that what she's worrying about?

"Perhaps. Ask me again if that ever happens. If I haven't gone yet."

The Walk is our euphemism — not even a good one. We're immortal, but we can die; we can be killed. As far as any of us know, this planet is half fire and molten lava, half sheer ice, while we inhabit the narrow strip that separates the two. If we leave the steam-zone, go too far in one direction or the other, the temperatures kill us. If the weather, topography, or giants don't kill us first. So when our kind decide to die, we Walk.

I keep a tally of choices: who goes to fire and who to ice, as though we cast a vote in death about which side will ultimately end the world. Thus far, ice leads by a small margin.

The ground shudders and shakes beneath us. Kyalikkeh grabs me to keep from tumbling down the mountain. The world wars with herself. I await the day she finally has enough and takes her own Walk.

"You know," Kyalikkeh says, relinquishing me as the tremors fade, "some days, it's like you'll go any moment. Then others, I can't imagine you ever will."

"Where would be the fun in that?"

She knows I don't like talking about this.

"In what?" She presses. "The Walk? Staying? Or predictability?"

"Our whole lives have become so predictable. Why should I wish to make it any more so?"

For a moment, the steam clears, blown by an errant gale, affording us a clear image of the battle below. The plates of my shell rasp against each other as I stand.

"It's nearly done." The land where they fought is ruined. What little life such an environment sustains will have burned to ash, then frozen in obsidian ice. In a few days' time, after the thaw, it will grow once more. The life of this time flourishes and decays at a rapid rate, desperately doing all it can in its short, short span. I sometimes find that pathetic and sometimes heroic, but always tragic.

"Should I tell the others to move camp now?"

I consider the question as we descend. "No, we should be safe for a bit longer. We'll wait until we've exhausted the food."

Chartreuse fog rises up to meet us. Where the steam meets the mountain, a line of psychedelic color begins. Tiny button fungi in blaze orange — a kind of mushroom — send up scarlet puffs of spoors. Electric blue cubes look like stone, but they're soft and absorb moisture from the air like a sponge, peek between the feathered moss-grass that shades from hot pink to royal purple.

The flora grows larger the closer we come to the mountain's base. We can still hear the echoes and feel the rumbles of the giants' battle, but here we are far from the last, desperate moments of violence.

Down here, the trees stretch two and three meters tall — delicate skeletal things that will never know what a leaf is. I brush too close to one and a branch shatters, coating me in fuchsia dust. I curse and brush as much off as I can. Kyalikkeh helps. If the clinging dust hardens, I'll wake up tomorrow with a new tree rooted and growing from my shell.

We come to gigantic boulders that centuries ago snapped off the mountain to tumble, crash, and ring down, into the valley. It jolted us all from our sleep, and nothing so unexpected has happened since.

The boulders had settled and snapped apart in fibrous, needle-like pieces that can pierce even my burled shell. Within the hollow created here by a few of those boulders, the all-pervasive steam hesitates to enter. As the pod's camp, it is perfect.

"You're back!" Kikkret races towards us, dodging crystal spikes and spurs by millimeters. I swallow my cry — his recent molting has left the shell too soft for such recklessness. Kyalikkeh doesn't even twitch.

He skids to a stop before us. "Kya, Tali — welcome back!" It's always strange to hear my name shortened, but he's my favorite, next to Kyalikkeh, so I let him. No one else, just him.

"Who won?" He peppers us with questions. "Are you going to see the giants now? May I come? What will you teach them, this time?" He's the youngest of us, a child in a world that no child deserves to inherit. But he hasn't learned that yet. For now, everything excites him with the promise of adventure.

My head waves back and forth. I can barely keep up; he makes me feel old.

"It's fire's win," I explain. "Ice won't be ready for a few hours, at least."

The fire giants are ready to see me immediately after a

loss, but ice takes longer to reach a state where they won't kill me on sight.

Kikkret sidles between us so his shell clacks against ours as we navigate the path. "Tell me again why they fight?" His favorite question for the last decade. I no longer answer, so Kyalikkeh does. I envy her patience.

"Fire wants more territory; half a planet isn't enough for them. And ice hates fire."

"And everything else," Kikkret supplies in a sing-song he uses when quoting someone — me, in this case.

"You'll learn to be a cynic, yet," Kyalikkeh informs him, while one eyestalk swivels disapprovingly in my direction.

I don't hear the music until just before we reach the camp. They play softly so as not to attract attention from the giants. They tap and slide along the crystals, producing an eerie sound that reminds me of long-vanished whales.

Kikkret joins the musicians while Kyalikkeh is called to settle a dispute and check on one whose shell we had to cut away where one of those fuchsia skeleton-trees began to grow from it.

There are eighteen of us left, and all except Kikkret and Kyalikkeh find my size intimidating. They leave me alone, and that suits me just fine. They all look like children to me, and the slightest bit alien with their six legs thicker, sturdier, their bodies bulkier, with their fore-claws and tail smaller. None of them remember when our race had the luxury to claim and defend individual territory, or battle each other on the ocean floor, back when this planet had saltwater oceans. 'Survival' means something else to us now, and I've never really understood what. But Kyalikkeh does, so I leave it to her.

Rather than join in the music or discuss medical advice, I check what our foragers found for food. Most of these don't remember a time when we ate meat, either. Many of them have never seen another living creature beyond the giants.

We have less than I anticipated. We have to move on, after all, and maybe give this area more time to recover before we return.

I tell Kyalikkeh, once she's finished with her patient, and she spreads the news through the camp. She leaves the musicians for last, waiting for them to finish the song because she knows how much I enjoy listening to them.

The trek to our next campsite takes half the day. It will take as long to reach my meeting place with the ice giants, so I leave the others to set up. Kikkret races after me, and I don't turn him away; I trust he'll return to camp when I tell him.

He plucks a vermillion frond veined in violets and turquoise from where it waves in a steam vent. After a moment of munching, he offers some to me. I never like to eat before meeting with the giants.

We travel mostly in silence, and I send him back when color begins to leach away, morphing from bold, vibrant hues to pastels. We're getting too close to ice territory for him to be safe. Even I have no guarantee of safety, and the giants at least perceive that I am useful to them — enough that most days they want to keep me alive.

The rime of frost draws a perfect line on the ground. The crystals crunch and crack beneath me. The line marks the outermost edge of the giants' territory. This is as far as most go — all except me and those taking the Walk into ice. This is a world of pale blues and grays, a stark contrast to the searing glow and charred blackness of the fire.

Frost gives way to perpetually falling, drifting snow. I can see where it clears ahead, becoming frozen, icy tundra. I won't go so far today; already, my joints stiffen. I move so slowly, I couldn't even evade a lumbering ice giant. Each of these visits is an exercise in trust: trust that today they will not forget what I have done for them. And trust that they have not learned of what I do for their enemies.

After another hour of waiting, one giant sees me and sends up a cry to its brothers. They crash towards me like huge, malformed gorillas.

They speak in creaks and snaps, and punctuate with showers of snow from their lungs — or whatever they have that passes for lungs. As languages go, theirs is simple.

They bellow their loss before they ever reach me. I wonder if they are more or less coherent to their fellows than they are to me. But I've been through this dance so many times before that I don't bother with translation. Timing is more crucial than meaning now, so I listen to their pitches and tone, count the bursts of icy white. It is always the same.

I open my bigger claw wide, lift the fan of my tail, but they don't notice. My claw snaps shut. The shockwave blows snow in their faces and pushes them back a step. Another plume of snow from my tail lifts as high as their heads. They fall silent; I have their attention.

"Of course those unspeakable beings," that is what they each call the other, as near as I can translate, "bested you. I have told you many times that merely repeating a strategy is no good. You need a new plan if you want to win the next battle."

"Teach us! Teach us!" They crow it like a chant whose meaning they have all forgotten.

I will — as I always do — if they agree to my terms, which they do. I bargain for territory. This sort of negotiation is tenuous, at best. If fire and ice have their way, the whole of our temperate steam zone would be so much black ice and dead sludge.

Their blocky heads tilt quizzically and I wonder why I bother with these things. I toss more snow, explain and shout and direct until my meat aches within the shell. Their jerky, stilted choreography looks enough like my intentions that I leave them to their practice.

I lumber from loose, hard snow to crunching frost, my body moving faster as it warms. I wish we hadn't needed to move the camp. It's still so far away, and exhaustion weighs me down. Then I see Kikkret racing towards me. Exhaustion falls away, forgotten. He should not be here. He heeds me better than that.

I will my legs to move faster, dropping to all six. We meet halfway. The blow from my claw knocks him tail-over-whiskers.

"When did you get so stupid? You were to return straight to the camp."

But he just lays in a heap on the ground. The clacking he makes breaks my heart, and now I know why he disobeyed.

"Who?" I hate this moment the most — the knowing without knowing. "Kikkret, who Walked?"

The string of sounds is as familiar as my own breath, but

it makes no sense. Not at first.

Then I hear it: "Kyalikkeh."

***

I don't return to camp. I can't. I return to my barren mountain, instead. Hours pass. Maybe days. What little meaning time had is now lost.

Foolish me. I thought I was prepared for anything. It doesn't seem possible that after so many centuries and millennia — loss piled upon the dust and exoskeletons of loss — there might be some untouched, unbroken part of me.

There was, but it's gone now. Taken the Walk with Kyalikkeh. I can't even hope to see her in the next life, because there is no 'next,' there is no more life. This is it. Not just the planet, but the universe is dying around us. There can be no more rebirth, and I'm not sure I believe in an afterlife.

Did she mean to say good-bye to me on the mountaintop? This mountaintop. How could she leave without at least a good-bye?

I would have stopped her. If not stopped, then at least I would have gone with her. Now, I'll never know how she cast her final vote for the world's end. Did she choose fire or ice?

We couldn't both leave. If it had to be one of us, I should have gone. She takes — no, took care of the rest. I just stir up trouble with the giants.

She and I have said so many good-byes together. We've had plenty of practice, but we never once said them to each other.

Had I gone first, I don't think I could have said it to her.

The shudders and tremors vibrating the mountain's crystal herald the start of another battle. I could finish my climb to the peak, watch the inevitable win as I always do, but as she's told me so many times, it's all pointless.

I wish I knew which way she went. Knowing would make joining her easier.

"Tali! Tali!"

Kikkret scrambles down the mountain, claws and legs wheeling, flailing to maintain his balance. I catch and steady him before he tumbles all the way down.

"You have to come see this."

"Not today. I'm not in the mood."

"But-but I think ice is losing. Shouldn't they win this time?"

Ice? Losing? In spite of myself, I let him draw me upward, to the peak. He tugs and grumbles when I don't move fast enough to suit him. Curiosity propels me forward. Curiosity that speaks with Kyalikkeh's sweet, familiar voice.

At first, I see nothing through the steam, though I haven't heard a battle this fierce in centuries. If Kikkret could pick out winner and loser from that cacophony, he may have a few things to teach even me.

Then a warm wind whips through the valley below, scattering chartreuse mist. I see what he means: ice defenses broken, in disarray, fire burning a swath of destruction through land I had considered for our next camp. I recognize the offense, in a way — a new strategy out of pieces of old ones.

"Am I right? Tali, are they losing? What's happening?"

"It would appear," the words leave me slowly, "that the fire giants have drastically improved their cognitive thinking skills."

A glimmer of true excitement. It's been so long since I last felt that. Did Kyalikkeh tell them? Did she give them this on her way out? As parting gift, as apology, that's the sort of thing she would do. But the lines and charges are clumsy, infantile. I'm not convinced it is her work.

Does it matter?

"Run back to camp," I snap the orders, "tell them to pack up. Move now." When ice loses, my territory negotiations will not hold. They may hold me responsible for this loss.

You are, at least a little.

Kyalikkeh's voice haunts me. She will haunt me until the day I Walk to her, but today is not that day.

The 13th Four-Leaf Clover

K Orion Fray

From the dawn of time, man has sought to control the powers that he finds in the world. Humankind tamed the fire—tamed the beasts—claimed the skies only to fly on to claim the moon. Science grew and flourished with the humans playing with it like tinker toys; the first tinkerers watched their work come to life on its own and called it magic; the generations after knew their power too well and merely called the science theirs. Life and death became their tinker toys, children walking in the shoes of their gods and fathers, standing tall and refusing to accept anything less than everything they wanted.

And as they found, those who walk in the shoes of the gods are often led to where they live.

A rift was found, just beyond the explored land of the continent. A shimmering line rent into the sky, accessible only by boat…and not by a voyage for the faint of heart.

The first attempts to reach the rift were met with chaos. The world on the other side, the land these gods lived in, was not meant for mortal flesh. It became the place of rumors and tales: the Bermuda Triangle combined with the River Styx, a land where people traveled and left no survivors. Still, mothers sent their sons to explore that dreamed-of new world, and still fathers prayed their daughters would not choose that path, and still no boats returned from the rift.

The second wave was one of force. The gods had made themselves known to the humans, and they were now denying them any information. They had been shown a carrot too tempting to simply be denied. Now the world pooled its resources and went to war against the enemy they had not been permitted to see. Soldiers died by the hundreds—but this time, some lived to tell what little they had seen during the fight. No stories of mythic figures or booming voices, but signs that reminded them of ancient religious texts. One straggling rowboat found its way home with tales of a great thunderstorm, bright flashing bolts of lightning blinding against a pitch black sky. Others returned and kissed the sand on the shores, talking of pillars of fire taller than even the mightiest warships. And one lone sailor, only survivor of his mighty fleet, painted a picture of the rift, clean and elegant in its simplicity, but with a hellish vision of death and destruction surrounding it.

The religious swore that the Rapture was nigh, and a gate to Heaven had been opened. The political leaned where they could, claiming that it was the punishment of one nation or another and this was what the world earned for believing in whatever terrible thing they were lobbying against at the time. The skeptics stood in the middle, claiming the entire event was media spin and that nothing truly existed out there; this was merely another way of stealing taxpayer money.

And then She emerged.

And Her sisters followed Her.

Mouthpieces of the Gods, though not the Gods themselves, the Muses entered the world in peace. They wanted nothing more than to understand the children they had found...to live in harmony with the humans. Three women, graceful and slender, beautiful and terrifying, as if mythology books had risen to life and walked among humanity...and all they wanted was to be mother and aunts to the human race.

They were captured, analyzed, and made into factory workers, nothing more than spirits to feed the buildings that housed them.

Three separate buildings, three towers in the center of the largest city they could find. Tall, so that the gods were close to the sky and distant enough from the humans to make the people below feel safe. A window in each, overlooking the city and the people, but small enough so that they could not slip through them. Strong pillars of steel and concrete, bastions of power and command—nothing that the weak would think to trifle with.

Walls were lined with every known mythological deterrent, in hopes of keeping the powers in—and that they might have safety away from the women, if the worse should happen. Iron, rowan, hawthorn, garlic, steel, salt, sage, tourmaline—anything at all, and as much as possible. The humans tried to bend the Muses to their will. They tried to make them work for humanity, make them create what the world wanted them to create. They wanted domination, they wanted power, they wanted weapons and immortality and the world on a platter.

The Muses weakened in their cages, apart from each other for the first time in their memory. They faded—literally and figuratively—until one brave man came and spoke to one of them, asking what could be done to help. He had heard the stories as a child; surely beings such as them who had come over some fifty years past now would not have arrived to sit in cages?

Fifty years. It had been fifty years. And the Muse smiled, and she bestowed upon him the knowledge he had requested.

Inspiration was the eldest of the three sisters, delicate and fragile as a sugar Easter egg but tall and beautiful as a sunset. She was in the highest tower, despite insistence that she was the weakest of the three sisters. In truth, she was anything but, though alone, none of the sisters truly claimed to be strong. Next in line was Creation, a head shorter than Inspiration with a curved frame like the waves just before a storm over the ocean. Even after all these years confined, Creation had a smile for everyone who approached her, and never complained as that smile turned translucent.

But Luck… Luck was the one who had found the scientist desperate for answers and brave enough to speak to her, and given him the strength to begin putting things to right.

Luck was the youngest and perhaps the smartest of her sisters, standing no taller than a human child with the youthful face to match. And it was she who leaned against the door, pale transparent fingers against the glass, and begged the man to build a new building. It did not have to be tall; it did not have to be guarded. It should be close to the land with a view of the world—the more of it they could see the better. And with all three together, they could revitalize themselves and the world around them…and send for the fourth Daughter of Fate, and show the humans all they had promised.

The scientist, and later the scientist's son, built the Muses their building. One story, with a view of the stars through skylights, the ocean from one window and mountains from the next. It was all they had asked for, and the man was blessed. The Muses gained in strength and formulated a plan.

And that was when they called for me.

I had not wanted to leave my home. My sisters were the adventurous ones, dreaming of new worlds and new opportunities. They had seen the rift between the worlds as a gift from our Parents, the Gods, as a new way to share our gifts. The humans were small and driven by greed, they told me. We can give them trinkets and allow them to believe they have control of their destiny. They do not know what they are playing with. We can give them this gift, and learn of ourselves together. Is this not better, sister? Could this not be what our parents wanted of us?

No, I thought. This was not what my parents had wanted of me. This was not what the Gods had given me my gifts for. I did not want to play the games of the humans. I wanted to serve my Parents, the Gods, as I always had. But my sisters had need of me. They could not play their games without me, and while they were patient to wait for me, the humans were not. Come, sister. Together we will play, and you will see how much these little children can learn.

They called. I answered. I was a faithful child of the Gods, and I would not leave my sisters alone.

The humans wanted power over destiny, my sisters told me, and so they had found a way to give it to them. Inspiration had taken a lock of Luck's hair and had Creation spin it into fabric, and with that they could create a pair of gloves. A snap of the fingers!—my sister clicked two fingers together—and the human world was changed. A stroke of luck, with a snap. A human gesture. A human idea. But even Creation could not make this fabric into clothing the humans could wear. No, the fabric of the Muses was too ethereal for the earth-bound humans they had come to serve. For that, they needed the one who walked the line. They needed the one who had allowed the rift. They needed the child who saw both sides.

They needed me—the Weaver.

I was a faithful child of the Gods, and I would not leave my sisters alone.

I stayed in their building, and wove their gloves. Now it was my turn to be the spirit of a factory, pulling at the strings of reality to bring what my sisters gave me into the world they had created it for. Day after day, I sat and made gloves, placing them into boxes for the humans to ship away. My sisters provided me reams and reams of fabric, and then spoke with the humans. A few officials were not afraid of them; the rare businessman stepped forward to see where these gloves were coming from. And still the scientist—for the scientists' son had become a scientist as well—stayed nearby, ensuring that my sisters were comfortable.

Once a pair of gloves had been made for every person, it became a process of watching the rise and fall of human life, and making a pair for each new person. At eighteen years of age, a human received their gloves. They now had control of their own fate, their own luck, and they needed to learn to conserve it. One pair was meant to last a lifetime—no new gloves were given. Humans could not wear the gloves meant for another.

The rules did not stop the humans from trying. Our building was sieged, my sisters and I attacked. Men and women attempted to force themselves onto us, to make us work for them specifically—making the gloves work for them, to make a second pair, to make them something different. But Luck was not on their side. She had made the bargain clearly, and would not change her mind.

After that first attempt, none made it to our home. There were not enough snaps in a pair of gloves to override my sister's Luck.

Years passed, and decades passed, and I watched my sisters marvel over the humans. Fascinated with their new powers, they tried their best to bend them—break them—to see how far they could push the rules of fate. Some learned that luck could only take them so far, and they perished for it. Riots erupted. How could you let them die? the signs demanded.

I gave them a stroke of luck, my sister replied. I did not make them immortal.

But if they had been lucky, would they not have lived?

If they had chosen their time sooner, they could have never fallen. But once in the air, there is no luck that can catch them. Perhaps they were lucky to land on the rock and break their neck, rather than to hit the water. Perhaps they died more quickly. Perhaps they died before they landed. You are not gods...you merely remind us of them.

No one was ever content. The luck was too much; the luck was not enough. The humans were not strong enough gods; the humans were dabbling too much in God's playhouse. We were saviors; we were hellions. We were a dichotomy in the world...and slowly, as so many other outliers which present too much of a conflict, we were eventually lost to time. No human had seen us in decades. The gloves appeared in their unique box, mailed from an unnamed agency on your birthday; the makers were nothing more than speculation and faerie tale. Spirits from across the sea? They were words for nighttime stories, not the reality of the world they faced. Why bargain with false spirits when criminals can simply have the fingertips of the gloves removed? Why act as if these have not always existed—have they not always been?

There were seven more sons in the line of the scientist before he returned no more. We had no need of sons or scientists, no need of helpers or watchers. We were self-sufficient, and best left alone.

I was the only one who wept for his departure. Because while we had no need of these things, he had been our most constant source of companionship. My sisters had each other. I did not.

But I was a faithful child of the Gods, and I would not leave my sisters alone.

...Even when they leave me alone.

But I continued to work. I took their fabric and made the humans into deities and I turned my face from the sky and the water and the mountains because I could not bear to look at the beauty. I could not bear to look at the world I was changing. For even sitting alone in my work room, I was changing the world, and my sisters could not see the changes they had made. We never can. We are all too close to the work that we do and cannot see its effect until it is far too late to make changes.

But I was the Weaver, and I must watch the threads of the world as these changes are made. I cannot stop them; that has never been my task. I simply must ensure that the threads continue to move, and tangle as little as possible. They will tangle, and many of those knots are built into the weave of Life, but some I can ease.

Some...I can ease.

Some.

I saw what was coming far before the others. They reveled in their game, in watching the toddlers learn to walk as we do, and stumble and fall. Creation was fascinated by the new and exciting circumstances the gloves had allowed the humans to make. Everything was new again, something she had not been able to see in many a lifetime. A new world with magic still just as bright and shiny as the first humans who had touched it had found it? There was nothing greater for her. She stood by the window with her arms stretched wide, soaking in the sun reflecting off the water and reveling in how much the world was still new.

Inspiration was alternately furious and transfixed by the humans and their minds. So often, they used their gifts for ill, and she would curse them and storm around the house. How dare they? They have so much of the world at their fingertips and this is what they choose to do with it? But then there were those who did something marvelous, and she would be in a state of bliss for days. The dreamers, the idealists, the visionaries made it all worthwhile for her.

Luck... I have never seen my sister so radiant. A Muse is always at her best when there are those who believe in them, and never had more people put faith into luck than did now. She stood before us all, beaming with inner light like I had never seen before, and just basked. What more could she do? The world had shifted to revolve around her; it was the wish of every deity to be loved—to be adored. My sister had fulfilled herself, and the others were content to sun themselves in her reflected glory.

They were too blinded by it to see. How could they have known? How could they have guessed what I had already seen for far too long?

More and more knots were appearing in my fabric—not the fabric Creation gave to me, but the fabric of the world we were in. Too many complications were arising. The world had not been built to handle this level of integration. The fabric could not stand up to so much meddling. The strands of the world have enough strength to take quite substantial blows—as we had seen when my sisters, and then I, arrived—but this...this was too much.

They grabbed for too much, they held on too tight, and soon, a snap of the fingers felt like a snap of a thread.

I tried to warn my sisters, tried to tell them that the world could no longer stand our presence. Could no longer stand the gloves, the twists of fate. I tried so hard to warn them that we had to leave and take our fabrics with us before it was too late. But they laughed at me. They pointed at all the marvelous things that had happened. How could it be too much? They are just beginning. They were so sure, so strong in their faith in the humans.

They could not see the humans losing faith in them. They did not remember the way that our world was made. Elysium, beloved and perfect, could not have been created that way. Even gods were once young, and Elysium was their home and playground. And children learn by falling and hurting themselves. We had once learned to harness our power through failures and tears. So had our Parents, and the Gods before them.

We were too young to see the creation of our world, but I...I could read it in the fabric. I could see it in the golden stains in the strings, the places where a Weaver before me had grabbed too tightly in hopes of saving something, and left remnants of their life-force behind in the threads.

And now it was our turn to fall.

I tried to slow it. I tried to catch the strings as they strained—broke—spun off back to the loom of the world to hang limply where no one could mend it again. Some I managed to tangle in my fingers before they left; some I wefted back into the fabric. Perhaps one out of a hundred, every year or so. But then they came faster. Then they snapped sooner. Then, my fingers bled gold with the strain of holding onto razor sharp threads as they desperately claimed freedom of the work I had done for them. I watched as corners of their tapestry came unwoven, began to fall into shimmering dust on the floor of the void. I watched, as only I could do, as the pattern rent down the middle.

I watched, for someone must witness the end.

The governments came for us, demanding answers. The gloves had begun to act erratically. Pairs which had been worn out for decades suddenly flared to life—of their own accord—but worked against their owners. The factories shipping out the gloves had stalled for weeks at a time, only to flare back to life in great explosions; quite literally, towns had been demolished by the surges of energy. People had been hospitalized because their gloves had given them too much power and had burned their hands. Others wishing for small salvations had been granted devastation. My sisters begged for time. They were just as confused as the rest of the world. They would look into it. They would fix it. They would ask.

And they came to me, and they demanded answers of me. Why was this happening? It was my job to watch the worlds, to ensure the safety, to keep the fabric intact. Why was I failing them? Why was I being lax in my duties? Simply because I did not need to "play catch-up" with production did not mean I could be lax in my other tasks! I was a Weaver, was I not? I was the Weaver for this world, and the world was coming undone! Was it not my task to keep the world whole? Was it not the one duty I was good for, and I was failing to live up to the promise my Parents had made me for? I was clearly not doing my work, and so—what was I doing?

…What was I doing?

I am a faithful child of the Gods, and I would not leave my sisters alone.

But I would not answer them. I wept, and I worked, and I watched the fabric stain with the gold of my life-force, and I watched. And as my sisters opened their eyes and watched their sunrise turn grey and fade, they knew. As they watched the trees turn grey and brown in the midst of the warmest season, they knew. As they watched the humans run out of luck with a fresh pair of gloves, they knew. They knew they had pushed too much. And they were scared.

I was no longer scared. I was empty, and sad, and alone.

My sisters barricaded themselves into their building. The armies came, and not even Luck could save us. We fled to the mountains, searching for the place where we had come from, searching for the rift. I could not lead them. I could not see the difference between the rifts that they had made for themselves against the one we had made at the first. The world was in tatters and I could not mend it fast enough to see what was us and what was them.

My sisters cried for their fate. Inspiration ran herself ragged looking for an answer, and could find none. Creation tried everything she could think of, looking for ways to make a new rift, a new way to go home. But the world was too worn and frayed to withstand another tear in its fabric. She could make a rift, but not one to home.

And Luck…sweet, innocent Luck was borne on the shoulders of her sisters as we walked. Once so beautiful and radiant, now she was so weak she could not stand on her own. All three grew pale, but we could barely see Luck now. She had given so much to this world, and now…the world was running out.

She had given so much, my sister. She had wanted these people to love her, love her gift to them. But you cannot give all of yourself to anything without risking losing everything in return. And now we were losing my beautiful sister.

It made me mad, watching her fade. Yes, my sister could be cruel, and yes, she could play sleight-of-hand with truth along with the best of them. But this had been her moment. This had been her chance to grow and shine…and it was being stolen from her. It was being taken by our sisters, who had wanted nothing more than to capitalize on the world they found.

It served them right. They had come to use the world, and now the world was using them.

When we found the cavern with the view of the horizon, my sisters turned to me. Creation begged, Inspiration pleaded. If any can free us, it is you, Weaver. And it was true. I could weave a door to our home and return through it, but...I knew that they could not. They were no longer strong enough to withstand the shift of the worlds. They had wrapped themselves too tightly in the world of the humans, and there was no room left for the otherworldly in them.

I could not look into their eyes as I told them. I could not watch their hearts break as they learned that they could never return to our home.

Then you go, Weaver, they urged me. Something can be saved of this world. Take what we have learned, and return it to our home. Do not let our deaths be in vain.

And I walked out to the edge of the cavern, and looked out at the receding ocean. I watched the edges of my vision sparkle as the fabric of this reality frayed and unwound and vanished before my eyes. I watched as the sapphire ocean and the azure sky and the ivory clouds and the emerald foliage all faded to a dull flat grey, and then to nothing at all. I watched as our little children, all the members of this brave new world we had found, screamed and rushed to avoid the oncoming void. I watched, and I listened, and I breathed.

Luck was gone now. Inspiration could no longer speak, her voice caught between anguish and the grave. It was Creation whose voice reached out to me now, soft and plaintive in its pain.

Will you not go, sister? Your time runs short. Our youngest is gone. You must save yourself.

I closed my eyes, to her—to the world—to the fading light. I took a breath.

And I smiled.

"I am a faithful child of the Gods, and I will not leave my sisters alone."

From Stone to Sky

Ross Bennett

Its favorite would be coming out soon. It always preferred the younger ones. The ones with skin that had never been marred by light falling from the open sky. The taller always seemed to be looking up while exploring the tunnels and caves they had so casually invaded, which turned its warnings of sprinkled dirt atop their heads into something to be cursed instead of praised. It stopped giving warnings, and some died in tunnel collapses. And yet, they kept looking up.

The smaller ones never looked up, and it always loved them for that. They kept their eyes firmly on the cave floors while wandering, and thus never needed to be warned about sudden drops or deadfalls. One of them sometimes left gifts of their strange, stiff food-bricks in the caves for it to find, and in time became its favorite of them for that. The first time it had found one, it had thought the tribute was simply an oddly-colored stone. Only after hours of puzzling over the slightly crinkly square did it realize that it could be broken open to expose some of the hard, tasteless food they seemed to prefer. It would never understand the fixation on bland, textureless food, but a sacrifice to it was still a sacrifice. It never forgot the smaller one who first did so.

It made sure things went better for them. Learning that the smaller ones were just younger versions of the taller took it time. Watching its favorite slowly grow taller and begin to look like one of its taller kindred was unnerving to say the least. Still, the young one kept leaving tribute for it, and thus it kept protecting them all. The price had been paid, though its patron never seemed to leave her tribute in the same place. Funny, almost as though the young one didn't know that the tribute would buy more if properly prepared in the same spot every time. Did no one know the rules anymore?

Over time, the favorite's actions began to become a matter of concern to it. The young one (for it would always think of its favorite as the young one, now) seemed unhappy to see its offerings missing. It would spend hours following its favorite human while she meandered through the tunnels and caverns, head hanging in what must be sorrow. Hours were spent aimlessly wandering through silent passages in the rock while it listened to the small one talk aimlessly about anything. In exchange, it would make sure those aimless feet would wander through cathedrals of stone that would usually have been marveled at.

Sometimes its favorite would stop and marvel. Mostly, it just seemed sad. So great was the favorite's displeasure that it began trying to learn about these interlopers. This was unheard of - never before had it cared to find what these humans cared for beyond the shine of some rocks or safe return to their open skies. They hadn't looked for open skies for ages, so something must have changed.

It paid attention to their wanderings, if only to protect them. It watched their slow meandering through caves and the ways they harvested edible things. They often managed to do so quickly enough that it seldom had time to react. In time, these incursions into it territory caused it to finally notice their slow creep into its tunnels, hewing them from its domain with the cruel steel blades of mankind.

It had grown angry, then. Ignoring its aid could be understood, but theft is theft between mortals and Fae alike. It began to take them in retribution, sending cave collapses or sudden floods to claim its tribute in their blood. They began leaving their domain only in groups. This did not dissuade it in the least. It carved through them with increasing wrath.

It was only when it realized that its favorite had not been seen in some time that it realized the flaws in this particular plan.

It retreated into brooding. No lives were claimed for weeks. Caves and food and shiny things were stolen with impunity. It did nothing about this, as it was far too busy hiding in the deepest inaccessible recesses of its nearly endless warrens. More weeks passed than it paid attention to.

Then it had come back, prepared to rage until it was given what it wanted. If it had to tear its way into the homes of the humans, through the huge vault doors that protected them, it would do so. It had chosen a favorite, and it would have her one way or another, and it would leave the consequences to the departed gods to sort out.

It was more surprised than it had been in ages to see its favorite running past those doors and almost into its open arms. Moisture ran down the girl's face like shale after a rain, and she seemed not to be paying attention to where she was running. The must have been running on nothing more than instinct. Her sure feet danced over the stone in a way that made it swell with pride - she remembered what it was to run through its home!

Minutes passed while it followed her from the domain of her kind and into its territory. More passed before it realized that it was being followed as well. Sharp footfalls resounded off rock to its ears, along with the occasional curse and stumble. It ran past her in its moment of confusion at this realization. She had tucked herself against the wall to catch her breath, thinking herself safe from those in pursuit. She proved to be far less talented at hiding than she did at running.

This was... A very new situation. Never before had it seen one human treat another like this - two of them lifting a smaller one from her feet and bouncing her shoulders and head off of the rough-cut stone of the cave. Only when she gasped in pain did it realize why this had been done. It knew enough of their language to listen and try and figure out what under the Earth could possibly be happening

The one of middle height spoke first. In moments it decided that this male was as useless as the rest of the sun-touched. Its voice was unpleasant and it was still holding her to the stone of its caves by the throat.

"You should have just let me have my way, little Mira. I could have made you like it."

Mira! It had a Name for its favorite. This had already become a moment to remember.

Mira managed to turn her head to meet the gaze of whichever one had just spoken, with an expression it didn't know nearly enough to understand. The voice it had so enjoyed humming or singing to herself was coarse, perhaps from the hand on her throat to keep her pinned to the wall, and the tone was curiously sharp. "None of your other girls liked it, *little* Sobei. Why should I be any di..."

Its eyes widened, as she was cut off by being bounced off of the wall by the one she had spoken to. So surprised it was that it took entire moments to realize that it had been given a Name for the first human it had truly hated in its entire existence.

"That was stupid of you, little Mira. Very, very stupid. Now I am not certain we will *ever* find you, out here in these tunnels. Easy for a scared little girl to get lost in here, da?"

It knew enough to see the threat for what it was, but couldn't get past the insult. She had never once been lost in here - it had been sure of that! She was its favorite, how could it let her come to harm?

The stone around them was already responding to its mood. Mira's eyes widened in understanding at the thin trickle of dirt dusting down atop Sobei's head from above in the only warning he was likely to get. She knew. Of course she knew. It's why she was its favorite.

Sobei and his lackey clearly didn't know the warnings. They were far, far too busy throwing Mira onto the floor and trying to pin her in place.

As always, some of the things these humans did made only the most tangential sense to it. Disputes in its world were handled by a sharp flow of stone, either swiftly eliminating the issue or to give the wrongdoer time to repent their sins in the darkness before silence took them. This haphazard flailing of limbs seemed odd. Clearly it worked for them, though. Mira made good her escape with both a sharp motion of her foot into something that must have been sensitive, and incredibly skillful use of the opportunity she had made for herself. Then she was off down the tunnel at a dead run once more.

It followed as stealthily as it had been, leaving her assailants to pick themselves up. It was only once it and she found themselves in a dead-end cavern that it wished that it had made good on his threat and brought down the cave to bring a final end to this chase.

It expected her to take some time to figure out that the cavern had no way out. Thus, it was incredibly surprising to find her doubling back. Surprising enough that for a moment, the beam of her head-lamp fell upon him. It recoiled with a sharp hiss at the artificial daylight, and she flattened against the cave wall and searched for him with light and eyes, while he hid from the direct, burning rays. It knew she didn't mean to hurt its eyes, and forgave her immediately.

She seemed scared by it, but she kindly learned that it ran from the light, keeping her head turned to grace him with her glance out of the corner of her eye. Her voice was soft but urgent, and filled with a sort of wonder that brought him out of hiding for her. "Oh Gods, you're real?"

Somehow it caught the question in her tone as well, and worked to turn its own voice to producing sounds that she could possibly understand. It managed to be confused, despite its lack of practice. "Of... course I am?"

She turned to look for just a moment, then realized that she was hurting it, and looked away once more. Still, she reached out to touch it as best she could. "My dzia was right. There are things living out here in the mines. I can't... I can't believe it."

It was too busy being stunned that she was not running. Humans always ran from it. This is how things ought to be. Yet here again she was not running from it, and in so doing she earned its protection.

She probably ought to have kept sprinting, though. Her pursuers found them at that moment.

At least, they found her. Something about the human mind tended to make them not notice it unless they were specifically seeking for it. These two were far too occupied with their quarry. In fairness, its attention was fixated entirely on her as well in its attempt to discern what exactly she would have it do.

Mira was far too caught in her sudden shock and fear to notice the scrutiny. Perhaps it was having her moment of realization that its existence wasn't a mirage sullied by the presence of her assailants that stole her words away. Her empty hands lifted as though to stop their approach, stepping slowly backward away from them and deeper into the dead-ended cavern as though she had forgotten that there was no useful reason to do so.

One long, unending moment passed before her glance twitched to it, pleading for help or intervention. Its choice was easy and fast. It made a sharp gesture and the top of the cave shifted slightly. Warnings had been given, but neither of her assailants even used what time they had to look up before tons of stone came down atop them.

Her scream stunned it, then filled it completely with confusion. It had given her exactly what she had wanted, hadn't it? Protection from her assailants. She disappeared down the path during its confusion.

It thought during its search. After all, she had nowhere to run, so it could take its time. What caused her to run from it? How had she been paying tribute and how had she known to talk to it without knowing that it even existed? Even more worrisome was how did no one else acknowledge its existence?

The only question it managed to answer before it found her was if it would help her more. She understood it, if only slightly. Thus, she had to be saved. It would get her out of this cavern, though it had no idea what to do then. Soft sobbing led it to her where she was hiding as best she could in the convolutions of limestone, while water ran down her face as it did over the stone.

Its questions left it then for a time, as it reached out of the darkness to brush away one trail of water from her cheek, surprised at the minerals in it. She flinched, but did not pull away from it. Or she tried, and was brought up short by the cool stone behind her head. It didn't specially matter, though. It didn't know how to make its voice any softer than the grind of granite on granite, but it did its best. "How and why do you bring water forth from your eyes, little one?"

She had her head-lamp off, but managed to look up and meet what passed for its face, gemlike eyes shining in the darkness. "You killed them, didn't you mister Karzelek? That cave-in was no accident."

It would have stammered, if that was something that it and its kind knew to do. Instead, there was simply a long pause of confusion. ".... Of course I did. I warned them. You saw me warn them. You *asked* me to. Why do you resent what you have been given?"

To her credit, she actually blinked. The limestone-white skin which had never known sun warmed to soft pink in sudden shame. "I... I asked you to? How on... Under Earth did you know that?"

Once more, soothingly cool digits traced that odd discoloration. "Sweet child, I have known you since you came into my caves on your mother's back. I can tell what you think, maybe better than your own father."

Time mattered less to it than to most. For her, the moment seemed to be unstuck in time. The question fell from her lips as though in a dream. "These are all your caves, aren't they? Anything past the bunker doors is yours, isn't it?"

It dipped its head in what it had learned meant assent. "They are, yes. All of them."

She struck it. She STRUCK it. It didn't matter that an open hand striking stone hurt her more than it hurt it. It didn't matter that it was incapable of feeling pain. She struck it, and it reeled to try to catch up. She was screaming.

"You killed them! YOU KILLED THEM! Family, friends, all of them! How could you! I gave you your tribute!"

It actually learned to stammer, just for its response. "I... I gave them the warnings! The trickle of dirt, the grinding of stone that always, always comes before a cave-in. You helped buy those, Mira. Only you.. only you seemed to care. And they didn't listen. They never listened to me. Why are you mad that they never listened?"

She wasn't listening either. Her hands hid her face, with shoulders shaking in sobs that it did not understand, no matter how it tried to. Hands brushed her own, its voice little more than a soft mumble. "Come, child, please. Please stop leaking. I don't understand why you leak from the face."

Her hands rubbed over her face, digging the heels of her palms into both eyes. Only then does she lift her chin to try and meet his eyes in the dim light of the faintly glowing fungus on the walls. "Oh, mister Karzelek, this is called crying. We do it when we hurt, not that you'd know that." One of those delicate hands reached out to brush beneath one gem-eye. "You must feel so little, but I think there was a reason you did as you thought I asked, yes? More than that I left you your food-gifts?"

It experienced happiness at that, drawing back and straightening up and offering her its hand to stand up. "Yes, child. Of course. How could I not?" It may have been shock, or that she was returning to the absurdity of learning that magic exists, but her hand slipped into its own and she stood up with its assistance. She even allowed herself to be led to the bare limestone face at the dead-end of the cavern.

"Come, little one," the humor escaped it, as she was perhaps as tall as it, "let me get you home." The wall began to weather under its will, passing through hundreds and thousands of years of the passage of water under its will, opening a path for them inch by inch.

She was not watching, clutching the hand of her guide and speaking, with enough agitation that even it became aware of it. "No! Not back there. Sobei and Feliks's friends will think it was me." Her voice caught. "They will think it was me that killed them, not you. That I hit them with a rock or pushed them down a hole and left them to die. You are right, mister Karzelek. Not many think you exist. There must be some other place I can go?"

The passage out was finished by then. It took some time to think, then led on. "Yes. Yes there are places I can take you. Come, child."

It led her down paths that only it knew. When there was no path, it made one for them with no tool other than its will. She followed, with the slowly dawning realization that she knew none of them. Yet she was not scared. Her imaginary friend was not imaginary, and though some part of her was constantly thinking that she had hit her head on a rock while running, she wanted to see the dream through to the end. After all, if her skull was cracked, then why not enjoy the fever-dream before life fled?

At first, it found for her the place it had hidden from humans for an age, or more than an age by this point. If anything, the shine of infinite facets of diamond only served to convince her that she had finally slipped into madness or the exhaustion of the walk.

Her face shone back at her, reflected on infinite angles of perfect crystals, lit in the soft green of bioluminescence. It knew from years past that this was what humans came into the stone to find - the wealth of the earth, carefully preserved in one shining, natural vault. "All this for you, Mira. The one who listens when others do not."

She stared in wonder for minutes. Walked the space, trailing fingertips over the stark beauty of infinite facets as though lost. It practically glowed in pride at having found a human to bestow its treasure upon, in return for the suffering it had failed to prevent. This was more than fair exchange. This, no human had been shown before, and she seemed to appreciate the chance for what it was.

"I'm thirsty, mister Karzelek. Can we keep walking?"

It was stunned. She was more interested in a drink than in its gift. A moment of rage passed through it, borne of confusion at being so rebuffed. Their location kept it from mistakenly sending a thin stream of dirt down her back. There was no way to cave *this* place in, and that gave it long enough to realize how disastrous that would be. It could not hurt her without doing more to itself.

Then it found itself laughing. The sound was for her benefit, but the mirth was its own. At her, for her innocence, and it for its own presumption. Once more it offered to lead, and she accepted. "Of course, small one. I will take care of you."

***

It found her water, dripping through the stone into

trackless pools of perfect glass in the darkness. Never once did she turn her lamp back on, and never once did it flinch from her scrutiny, intense and direct as only the small ones could be.

It found her food - dozens of the wrapped rations that her kind seemed to subsist upon. She took what she could carry, but insisted upon continuing. It did not understand. The store room it had found for her had enough to feed her for a lifetime, yet she was scared of it. It protested, but she led it along as forcefully as she could. It humored her and let her push it along, though of course she could not have moved it if it did not let her. Only once around several turnings did she speak.

"Why did you show me that, mister Karzelek?"

It paused and regarded her, though it did not let the pace slow. By now it had learned that she hated that. "You hungered. I found you food. Is this not as you wished?"

Her hand was shaking, and the other clenched around her reclaimed food packets. "Did you not see the dead, there? The piles of them"

It thought back to the space, and the odd jumbles of calcium sticks in piles through the space. "Your dead become stone? They become as I, but unmoving?"

She gave that laugh that filled it with the desire to protect her from all things. "Oh, you silly thing. How have you watched us for so long and learned so little?"

It thought for quite some time. "Never before did I care to learn, child. You were the first of your type that I considered mine."

She smiled then, and it was pleased.

***

By now, she was leading. She had learned to judge which caves were safe, and where to find water, as if she was learning its sight through simple proximity. Only rarely would it turn her from certain paths with a gentle hand. It had never once returned to its old caves. She was with it, and none of the others had even cared that it existed. Weeks of walking and talking with her had taught it that it felt sorrow at that. Sorrow that its existence was no longer known among mankind, and that none cared to learn.

Then, as all children do, she escaped its guidance and found one of the long, smooth passages it kept her from. It chased her around unnatural right angles carved into the stone, while she skipped ahead, laughing in the joy of exploration that had endeared her to it before she even knew to leave gifts. She made it out of its reach just before it could stop her, and stopped dead, transfixed by her first view of a sunrise down the long-forgotten mine entrance.

Its voice was soft, and it was caught between reaching out for her and recoiling at the pain of the sun's heat. "Please, Mira. Please come back?"

The sound of its voice snapped her out of the spell of the sky, and she darted back into shadow to embrace it. It did its best to mirror the gesture - she had been teaching it to hug for days now.

"Oh, Mister Karzelek! I knew you would take me up here sooner or later, but I just couldn't wait! Is that really the sky? Really the *sun?*"

It nodded mutely and did not let go. "Please don't go up there, Mira. Please? Stay here with me. You don't have to go."

She smiled and tightened her embrace around it. "They said it was safe, now. All the bad things were gone from the sky, if only we could find our way back out. And now you've shown me! I can't thank you enough."

It shook, and the stone of its mountain shook with it ever so slightly. "I can't go with you, child. You know I can't. Please don't leave me yet? You're too young. You're not ready."

She smiled, and made a gesture it had not seen before. Her lips brushed its face, just beneath an eye. "You can't truly make me ready, Mister Karzelek. It's time I went up and saw the sun."

It had no reply. All it could do is let her go out of its reach, to a new life all her own. And somewhere beneath the sensation of loss, it learned a new facet of pride in its favorite child.

Silver Linings

Kate Larking

When I opened my eyes for the first time, I only saw blackness—snow and ice pressed against my face. Chills raced up my arms and chest, down my legs. I lifted myself up—a strange sensation, light and floaty compared to my previous landlocked state. My view of the snow changed to a white, crystalline imprint of my face.

"There's a good girl."

I blinked, staring at this imprint. Was that me? Really? Narrow-nosed, high cheek bones, thin lips. I waved my hand before my face. The cream-coloured fingers, impossibly pale yet so rich against the background of ice and snow, snagged in my dangling hair. The hair wafted like spider webs lining a cave's entrance. I made a noise, low and glottal, foreign yet humming inside my body like a close friend.

"Who knew you'd be so pretty?"

I looked up into the rich brown face. A faery? She had to be, with her ears pointed like the ground gremlins, not softly curved like human explorers I'd occasionally spied upon. Faeries rarely ventured to my poles—the underwater North or the cold-locked South.

She smiled with tiny, pointed teeth, and tucked her long blonde locks behind her ear. "How does it feel, to be given form?"

I touched her cheek, my fingers quivering and clumsy against her smooth skin. I shuddered a breath, but strength seeped through my fingers, into this faery. I collapsed into the snow.

***

I don't recall much from the first year. The next time I could really understand that I had human-like form, the faery—Stepphie, I knew her name now but I don't remember when she introduced herself—and I lived in an apartment in San Francisco. I mostly lay in bed, under a pile of blankets Stepphie lovingly arranged around me, over me, beside me.

Stepphie presented me with a calendar, pointing out how every day she had added a tick to mark that I had lived that day. From then on, days would have two ticks. "You can't stay in bed forever," she told me with a smile.

Every night starting that evening, Stepphie, held my hand and we walked to the library through quiet, human streets. Under salmon-tinged streetlights, the concrete sidewalk reassured me, reminding me of the steady clasp of Earth around me. Twilight's darkness helped, too.

Once at the library, Stepphie opened the back door, the double steel more imposing than the sliding glass front ones. With no humans around at night, she shook a few stars from her pale hair. Floating around us, they provided just enough light pick out books and read.

At first, Stepphie sat with me in a corner, and read aloud from picture books. Most of the stories featured people smaller than their caregivers. I curled up to be as tiny as I could beside her slight frame when she read to me. Every dawn as we strode back to the apartment, I would watch over my guardian faery's head. Was I the one who should be protecting her?

When I picked up on letters, the books Stepphie selected at the library only had text, and then I was reading them. I stumbled over words, reciting the stories to my faery. Stepphie nodded along, like she had read all the books before.

***

When we had access to power, we watched television documentaries and news reports, most prattling about climate changes, polar shifts, melting and reforming ice caps. I understood that—something felt wrong with the Earth, off-kilter under my feet. But I was powerless to reach it; my body was now outside the geographic poles.

"You've been rendered, Pola," Stepphie explained to me shortly after we moved—again. She pulled the calendar out of her bag and perched it on the fireplace mantle open to June. The days had just begun to collect three ticks—my third year of…rendership? Renderdom? "It's a rare thing, for new entities to be born in this day and age, especially with so many humans on the planet. But enough of the fae decided to switch things up, so here you are."

I examined the lines of my hands. My skin had cracked in the dry, wintery air. June last year had been full of autumnal leaves falling from trees in Oregon. Once winter had descended on Portland in September, we moved to Vancouver. It felt like the winter eclipsing the world followed us wherever we went. Stepphie insisted on travelling; fall was her favourite season so she wanted to see it before winter stole it away.

"Isn't it supposed to be summer? The calendar says summer is starting." I clenched my hand and flexed it open. The thin coating of stiff skin didn't feel right. I tried to stop comparing it to being with the Earth—Stepphie made it clear that I couldn't go back, no matter how deep I buried myself into the ground, or how many blankets I piled overtop myself.

"Summer? No, not anymore. But, I have an idea!" Stepphie jumped to her feet and clasped her hands under her chin. "Let's go meet up the Winter Queen. She always has the most fun on the Darkland borders." Twinkling light danced in the faery's eyes and she nodded. "If we start moving now, we should be able to meet up with her in Calgary before the Darklands overtake us."

Winter Queen? I mentally flipped through all the books we had read about winter but no queen stood out. Human tales barely scratched the surface of what Stepphie knew.

Stepphie kissed me before she ran to jam her apparel back into her overflowing suitcase.

So, we were leaving again? True, the dead leaves were frozen on the trees in crisp brown curls. The Darklands would catch up soon, sentencing the city to a lengthy winter. Still, we rarely left cities before we had to use our snowshoes to wade out of snowdrift-covered city streets. I followed her to bedroom to pack, still clenching my dry, empty hand.

***

Sheet lightening flared across the sky as the sprites flared with anger. I glanced up at the whirling snowflakes. Thunder cracked overhead. "Thunder flurries again?" The clouds churned, sprites mingling in the puffy greys.

"It's happening more often." Stepphie's chunky-knit scarf muffled her voice. She gazed up at the sky, too. Her fine blonde hair tumbled out of the scarf's constricting folds and flared loosely with the static caused by the dry winter air. "The itinerants are used to seeing each other maybe once in a hundred years when their patterns meet up again." She snickered. "All those once-in-a-century, dramatic flings are catching up to them."

I kept staring at the clouds, their undulating greys obscuring the sun. More clashes, more lightning. "What was it that humans say about clouds having silver linings?"

Stepphie slipped her hand into her parka pocket and produced a book, a dog-eared idiom book she'd stolen from the library we inhabited in San Francisco. She offered it to me.

I took it with a sigh. She was going to make me look it up even though she could simply tell me? I flipped through the pages, scanning the bolded headings. When I found it, I read, "Silver linings: comforting or hopeful aspect of an otherwise desperate or unhappy situation."

"I doubt humans would say the same if they knew it was snow sprite excrement."

"There's a whole section in here about poop idioms," I replied, arching the book's back cover and scrolling through the pages with my thumbnail.

Stepphie snatched the book back—or tried to. I held it above my head, well out of her reach, continuing to thumb through the pages. I could almost make out the bristling of the translucent fur that blended in with her hairline. I'd learned how to push her buttons, mostly from the middle grade books at the libraries I would sneak to read while she was browsing encyclopedias on her own.

I grinned, then relaxed my extended arms.

She snatched the book back and stuffed it into her parka pockets then snapped the pocket flap in place. "Don't desecrate the book by hunting out the drivel."

I smiled. "Why is the Winter Queen on a ridge, anyway?" I kicked an iced-covered rock down the trail ahead of us. "You said she liked the rivers?"

Stepphie shrugged. "The rivers are more ice than water these days. If she wants to play with it, she has to dig for it."

We approached the rock and I kicked it forward again. It arched to the left, then off the packed snow path, and then over the ledge toward the houses we slowly rose away from. The houses below us looked like creamy desserts with their snowy tops and smooth curves at the iced roof edges. Not as many roofs had collapsed in this neighbourhood, but I could pick out at four, the splintered trusses jutting through a soft dusting of snow over the remains of colourful bedrooms.

"What if she asked the Earth sprites to channel her a water supply?" I wondered.

Stepphie tapped her chin with her mittened hand. She parted her lips to reply.

"I did. Those poor dears are permafrosted," someone ahead said, her clear, bored voice ringing over the snow and echoed into the neighbourhood graveyard below.

I glanced ahead. The white-lipped, teal-skinned Winter Queen sat erect in her ice throne, overlooking the ridge. She grinned at Stepphie.

"There you are, Majesty," my guardian said. "I had an inkling you'd still be up here."

"Perhaps my Calgary favoritism is too overt, if you can predict I'd linger here." The Winter Queen reclined on her throne. "Anyway, just call me Aurora, Stepphie. You and I have too much history for formal titles." The icicles backing grew slightly more, fanning out in fractals with the precision of a magnified snowflake.

Stepphie stopped before her and assessed the display. "Not your grandest work."

I inhaled sharply, then coughed as the cold stung my lungs. Stepphie had warned me that the Winter Queen was powerful—more powerful with the Darklands and ever-winter eclipsing the continent. Why would Stepphie criticize her so curtly?

Aurora sighed. "It's true, my dear. But when one doesn't have the constraint of the seasons forcing one to outdo oneself, thrones become a more mundane venture. I have all the time in the world to improve this one. Or I could build a new one there." Aurora turned, her black hair falling loose over her shoulders, and she pointed to the most modern of the ice-encrusted skyscrapers.

Now, they were stormscrapers, ruins of a human land overtaken by the elements. Even if the winter hadn't fully captured Alberta yet, the mountains expedited the snow-laden storms into Calgary.

I finished coughing.

Stepphie grinned and locked her jagged teeth into a feral grin, the look a sharp contrast to her usual sweetness. "I like the prospect of a skyscraper throne."

"An eternal view of an ice-locked city," Aurora murmured poetically. She, too, smiled and I saw the same malice touch her eyes. When she turned to me, she frowned like she only just realized I had accompanied Stepphie. Her shimmering eyes caught on me. "Oh, my. You brought a friend to play?"

Stepphie dipped into a curtsy, pinching the corners of her book-infested parka like it were a grad ball gown. "Aurora, this is Pola."

A snarky laugh tore from Aurora lips. Her eyes warmed in the presence of the Stepphie's light and reflected tiny prisms onto the white snow. "Stepphie the Exile accompanies the Polar Render! How grand! Oh, the Light court is such a laugh! You're relegated to the Darklands perimeter, living along the shred of light left on this side of the world, but they ask you to babysit?"

"Being with Pola was my own decision." She tilted her head back to smile at me.

I smiled, slightly, but my lips wavered more than curved.

"The Darklands chase you, then?" Aurora flicked the tips of her fingers at the western horizon where darkness cut through the mountain range.

Stepphie stood and I caught sight of the twinge of humour on her lips. "Always just out of reach." But she reached back to clasp my hands. "The plan is to travel the globe."

"Oh, delightful. Where are the Summerlands these days?"

"From what I've heard, the Light Fey are developing real estate on the New Dunes in East Africa. I hear development can be quite expensive since human labour dies out too quickly before any projects are complete."

"Perhaps if they did it themselves?" I mused.

"Oh but never, baby render!" Aurora drew a snow-speckled breeze to her, weaving it between her fingers. "I can imagine the dingy glass castles now. Human workers creating their refined glass—much more exquisite." She turned again to the stormscrapers and smiled.

A crunch of snow drifted to my ears, then another. Beyond Aurora's wind-fiddling fingertips, a coat-shrouded figure clomped along the trail ridge, hands tucked under his armpits. Ice frosted his white scarf, his eyebrows and eyelashes. Little puffs of fog trailed from his mouth. He glared out from under the brim of his red, knit hat.

Aurora followed my snagged attention and turned. She smiled. "How much longer do you think the humans will survive?"

The figure continued to trudge toward us in his too-large boots.

"Too long." Stepphie sighed.

I stared at Stepphie. Her face had stilled, even and calm even against the frigid wind. That frightened me more that her malicious grin ever would.

Aurora grinned and her fingers closed over the breeze twining around her fingers. She blew a kiss toward the hiking figure and the swirl of snowy wind rushed him. He toppled backward, thumping deeply into the snow as the breeze wrenched his red hat from his head. "What?" He flailed, trying to catch his hat, but Aurora's fingers moved like a conductor's and the hat surged up into the wind like a bulky bird.

Lightning lit the skies again as Stepphie giggled. I couldn't help but smile at her hypocrisy. Toss his hat away, no issue. But hold her book out of reach? The world would end. Or the world would end more quickly. Something like that.

The hat drifted overhead and fell to the ground a little ways down the trail Stepphie and I had slogged up.

The man scrambled to his feet and stared at us: a blond, child-like thing laughing at his hat-astrophy; an icy Winter Queen sitting back in a rather modest throne at a ridge's edge; and me. "Who are you?" He called, too loudly. The cold carried his voice to us clearly.

Thunder crackled overhead.

Stepphie turned to Aurora. "You gave him Sight? Really? Why?"

Aurora shrugged. "One does what one can for ones amusement in these times. There is no concern about remaining hidden now."

"Who are you?" The man called again, rushing along the path to stop near Aurora's throne.

"Us?" Stepphie tilted her head. "No one you cared about before now."

"Aren't you cold?" he gestured to her hat-free head, the fine gold of her hair rising around her face.

Stepphie shook her head and smiled. "Aren't you hot?" She pointed to his sweat-slickened hair that now collecting a few flakes of snow.

"Not anymore!" He grinned, too enthusiastically against the cold air. "What are you doing out here? Are you travelling sun-ward? Can I come with you?"

I examined his face, reddening cheeks and dark lashes. These are the people who threatened the total destruction of the fae? I glanced toward Aurora as she stood from her throne.

Aurora took two steps before the man turned to her. Then another one before his stare flicked to her naked teal feet in the snow. But a snap of magic and ice encrusted her feet from knees to toe, the ankle flexing with her movement like my soft leather boots did.

The man stilled. "What are you?"

"Just some faery type things." Aurora answered.

"Fairies?" The man scoffed. "Like the tooth fairy?"

Aurora clasped his chin and her fingers iced over his jaw. "I suppose I could be a tooth fairy." She grinned.

He blanched and snapped his hands around her fingers and the ice lining his throat. Another tendril of magic froze his gloved hands in place, affixed to his neck.

He screamed, an animal sound without his jaw to move it into coherency.

I stilled.

Aurora turned to me, her forehead still dangerously close to the man's doe-wide eyes. "This doesn't make you happy?" she asked me.

I shrugged as tears overflowed from the young man's eyes and melted a small gouge in Aurora's angular ice-hold. But the tears lacked strength to cause more damage and froze along his cheeks. Like a glazed donut, I realized. I turned to face the city. "I have limited experience with these things."

"She's not exactly fae, Aurora. In the Light or Dark sense like you and I." Stepphie trotted up to sit on the smooth ice wall extension of Aurora's throne. She kicked her legs out, swinging them back and forth like a child.

Aurora pursed her pale lips. "Ah, it seems I misled you, young man. She is not a faery. But I can't have you around to tell people that." She kissed the hysterical weeping man on the cheek. Ice filmed over his whole body. He stared at his hands and screeched, inhumanly, animalistically. He collapsed to his knees and the ice finished encasing him into a prison of angular prisms.

Aurora sighed and ran her hand along the iced-over, sweat-licked hair. "Humans are so pathetic." She harvested a glittering black vapor from the human with the action—fear.

"We didn't manage them properly, true." Stepphie gazed out at the ice city with a smile. "We shouldn't have let them develop to the level they did. Now we have to cull and force them to start over."

"If we didn't need such creatures to feed from, I would

have frozen them all a long time ago." Aurora inhaled the fear pooled in her palm. She turned back to her throne and flicked her hair over her shoulder.

I stared at the man. His skin pulsed under the ice. It was like he was sealed in the same plastic as the shiny new picture books Stepphie occasionally procured.

"Is she usually this intrigued by humans?" Aurora murmured to Stepphie, but my ears still caught the voice on the cold air.

"Yes. It's unfortunate." Stepphie called over to me, "Are you done looking, Pola? We are here to visit Aurora."

This city still had people in it, even as the Darklands approached? San Francisco had had human inhabitants, but they hadn't known the Darklands approached until it locked the city in ice one drizzly September. These ones, why were they here still? Struggling and striving to collect enough rations and supplies to make their way to the new Midlands where the sun still visited. With the Earth tilted, new habitable regions formed and old ones were destroyed.

"Why do this?" I touched the man's ice-covered cheek. Cold beyond cold, my skin threatened to stick to his prison. I retracted my curious finger.

"There are too many." Aurora strode over to me and took my hand in hers. "We must reset the balance of beliefs." To Stepphie, she muttered, "I thought you were teaching her."

"I do too teach her!" Stepphie snapped, jumping up off the throne to stand.

I shrugged. "Balance of beliefs?"

"The ways of the current world won't matter soon. Only words matter now as they create the base for knowledge." Stepphie lifted her dictionary from her pocket.

"She will still need to know how it was, Stepphie." Aurora shook her head. "The balance of beliefs is what brought you to be, dear Pola. Fey have a certain amount of belief, or sway, in the world. It's balanced out by humans, who have their own set of beliefs. While the fey live longer, we didn't expect the humans to decrease their mortality rate to a point where their belief cycle thoroughly outweighed ours. But the larger of a population they became, the less they believed properly." Aurora leaned up to look at the sky. More lightning flashed and she smiled, her white lips hauntingly stark in the sudden light. "They bogged themselves down in the way the world works, you see? All this science and digital life, mass production and electricity—it eroded their belief weight with logic. So we waited for humans to decay themselves from the inside. Humans now, as a whole, have very little belief left. The few of us fae left were finally able to act."

"Some disagreed," Stepphie chimed in, rocking back on her heels. "Like the Light court, for the most part. They wanted to maintain a reservation of humans. But enough in the Light court realized the selfish motivations of those who wanted to control the humans for their own gain. It only took a few Light defectors to skew fae belief into a resolution for action." She smiled broadly.

"Our belief that a polar shift would be the best way to alter this world is what brought you to be, Pola." Aurora wrapped her fingers around my jaw and tilted me to face her. "You are our mastermind. Our gift of rebirth to the world."

I pushed her away and she staggered back, frowning. "But how do you explain this?" I gestured to the frozen boy.

His eyes flicked to stare at me.

And I stared back at him. I swayed on my feet and he blinked, slowly.

Stepphie tilted her head. "Pola, Aurora's Dark fey. She eats fear. She doesn't care about one random human like this."

"And what if I do? What if I care?" I spat back. "What if I don't want to see this? What if I don't want this to happen? Unfreeze him."

Aurora grinned, a feral mixture of sweetness and obstinacy. "No."

Stepphie turned to Aurora. "Can you just do it so she'll be quiet, Aurora?"

So I'll be quiet? So I'll be pacified?

"I quite like him like that, actually. So, no. Pola needs to learn eventually. Enough of us believed in her that she showed up on Earth to play with us. We made her into a being—we can take it away if she causes trouble."

"If I cause trouble? Like what?"

Stepphie's eyes widened, just for a breath. She shivered, a slight tremble under her parka. If I hadn't been staring at her, I might not have noticed. Then she settled back to her usual innocent face.

Aurora stretched her hand out for me to take. "Come along, Pola. I think I might make that throne now. Would you like to see?"

I'd seen this. In human books and movies. Condescension, treating someone like a child. But if human children had power, a young render would have power, right?

I had power.

I grasped the boy's hand. "Just a moment," I whispered into his frozen ear. "Just hold on."

"Pola?" Stepphie stepped forward.

I reached into the Earth with my mind and plucked the veins of the plates marking the surface. So close to the darkened ocean and mountain range, the vein was nearby.

The ground quivered and heaved.

Stepphie wobbled and fell, bracing all fours on the ground. Aurora leapt into the sky and landed back on her throne. The ice boots froze into the throne to steady her.

I ripped open the surface, cracking through the permafrosted soil and down into the rock base. The boy and I dropped into the tunnel.

I slammed my back into the tunnel wall and held the boy on top of me. My clothes snagged and tore away. I cursed a word Stepphie would have smacked me for using.

The rocks scratched at my flesh but didn't break into me. We were the same. But the boy, he wasn't. I clung to him, holding him close enough that his frozen, jagged-edged body wouldn't snag on the roof of the tunnel but not so close to grind him into the ground speeding behind me.

"Smoother!" I begged of the Earth.

The tunnel groaned, louder than any sprite thunder, trapped in the ground. But as the tunnel broke before us, the walls smoothed. The pitch black tunnel turned in long gentle curves.

I heard it coming. The hiss of a storm breeze in a tight space, rattling through doors. One movie had a documentary of sounds and the humans had wobbled a metal sheet to make the same noise. The similarities were uncanny now, trapped in the darkness.

Pellets of cold flicked into my hair, freezing the tips. My face burned. Aurora, trying to stop me? Pull me back?

Lightning from the Calgary skies ricocheted off the frost slickening my tunnel's walls, lighting them with shining silver for an instant.

I reached up, into the freezing air and pulled, yanking the Earth to close after us.

The light vanished. The air stilled. We fell deeper and deeper and the air began to warm. Moisture bled into the front of my remaining coat.

The Midlands: that would be the sun-ward lands the boy wanted, right?

I leaned my foot into the tunnel's edge as we streaked through the tunnel. The Earth felt me, knew me. We curled and drifted, sliding through the Earth.

"A little longer," I whispered to the boy, my throat parched, but the rock closing around us crumbled obscured my voice into nothing.

It took longer than I thought it would, for us to find light. But when it opened ahead of us, I had no time to prepare.

The Earth spat us out against gravity. My grip on the boy fumbled and he slid free of me.

The Earth, closing too quickly, snagged my foot in its seal and I slammed, chest-first into the grass.

I groaned, but inhaled the rich scent of living Earth and moss and rain. The words in the library books hadn't done the fertile spring's perfume any justice.

I rose to my forearms. I was in a nest of overturned soil and uprooted plants. Green fields surrounded by a long, slatted fence. A farm? I pressed myself up and glanced around.

Against the rim of emerald grass to my left, the frozen boy.

"Shoot," I grumbled and stumbled upright. I flicked my

foot free of the clinging ground. "Thanks," I murmured to it.

The Earth rumbled, a soft sigh as it turned over in its slumber.

"Yeah, I'll try not to be as pushy next time. Sorry." I sunk down to sit beside the boy.

The sheen of ice encasing him dripped away, moistening the soil. His flesh even gave a little as I touched his pulse.

Nothing.

His dead eyes stared up at the blue sky, his lips parted and mouth still wedged open with block of ice.

But, I could have sworn his eyes had flicked back as we stood on that cliff edge. That he had blinked under the ice. That he had still been alive.

The ice had lied to me, warping my vision to play with my emotions.

Tears trickled down my face. I didn't like the boy. Not at all, really. He was naive and defective. He should have run at the sight of Aurora's teal skin. Humans usually retreat if they saw something off or different, right? Why hadn't he?

I sat back on my Earth, in the midst of my overturned dirt. The Earth cradled me, the soil infused with stone curling itself to support my back.

No matter what I did to the Earth, it still followed my bidding, no matter how extreme my wish. I sunk my fingers into the dirt. I could feel the reverberations as the Earth pouted. It chilled against my fingers for just a breath; it had missed me.

I reached with my mind, magnifying the reach of my fingers. Further and further I reached, a quarter of the way around the world, to winter-locked Calgary.

I plucked a chord of Earth.

The vibrations shook my arm into numbness. I closed my eyes, imagining that simple ice throne fracturing. The stormscrapers' windows shattering, glass shivering itself free of ice and rebar constraints.

A part of me wanted to destroy that idiom book in Stepphie's pocket from this far away. But had she really done anything wrong?

I stood. As I had drifted in the Earth's power, more ice

had melted from the boy. His jaw began to relax. I closed his eyes gently, careful to not break his still-cold skin.

Over the fields, I couldn't see any workers. But there was a house. Maybe I could start there, introduce myself and my situation. If they believed me, maybe I could... Maybe I could change this?

The Earth cooled under me. My breath caught in my throat. I fell to the ground on all fours. I pressed my both hands into the green grass, into the soil, fingers reaching down as deeply as I could.

Under me, the structure of the Earth had changed. The chord of Earth I had just plucked...it had moved!

It had been strung deep through the planet, one point locked on Calgary, the other deep in southern Indian Ocean, but it had shifted. No, it was still moving. The point that had connected to Calgary drifted, slowly, toward me. It was pursuing me, following me...

The Darklands. They followed me. I was the reason winter overtook the places Stepphie and I had been. My rendering hadn't changed what I was, hadn't granted me a powerless body for my consciousness to inhabit. The poles saturated my being, even now, in this humanoid form.

Stepphie had worked hard to distract me from the sad truth of our wanderings: winter followed me. I was the reasons the Darklands moved.

I slammed my power back into the Earth, summoning a tunnel, and dropped, slipping and sliding through the ground. The Earth groaned around me, complaining about my new shape, about my nonsensical desires.

"I'll never do it again," I promised in a whisper.

It spat me out, where I had left Aurora and Stepphie. Stepphie stared at me with sad eyes. She seemed so old, crouched on the ground, staring at the overturned snow-and-soil remains of my first tunnel.

"The poles chase me?"

"I didn't quite know how to tell you..." Stepphie sighed and frowned. "The sun wants the Light fey." She spread out her mittened hands. "But it can't have us back, now that we've been rendered. There are enough of us that it doesn't affect the world the way your singular presence does." She tried to offer a small comforting smile at the end.

Aurora, though, stared at her shattered city with her hands on her hips. "Honestly, why did you have to go and do a thing like that?"

I turned to downtown. The buildings had sloughed off their glass, lining the streets with crystalline shrapnel. Perhaps I had gone overboard with my childish impulse to ruin her plaything. I strode over to Stepphie and extended my hand down to her.

The smile wavered, but held. She clasped her mitten-covered hand in mine.

I helped her to her feet and hand-swept the dusting of snow from the backside of her parka. She blushed pink, her smile broadening as she eyed me over her shoulder.

I started down the slope.

Stepphie trailed compliantly after me.

"Where are you going?" Aurora called. "You only just got here."

I shrugged and kept walking. I swooped down a hand to pluck the red knit hat from the ground, and tugged it onto my head. No warmth remained in the knit.

"Pola?" Stepphie's voice was faint against the blustery winds. "What are we doing?"

"Hunkering down, I think. Waiting for winter."

The Shape of Things

April Steenburgh

There was a particular cast to the sky, right before a storm. Colors were skewed just to the side of natural, light seemed to be coming through a technician's filter. Clouds could slip and sneak, leading the unwary to believe nothing was amiss-they were too flat to suggest thunder, too thin to release a deluge. But they were the scrim that would pull suddenly aside as the thunderheads gave voice all at once and too close to run from.

The birds knew, those that were left. They would stop their tottering dance on the shore, desperately trying to avoid the surf while still seeking any bit of biological matter that might be left to ingest. They would pause, almost as one, and turn their heads towards the sea. It was a look of fear, and then the air would be filled with wing beats rapid and uneven as the internal rhythm of a cardiac patient, torn and broken feathers falling just ahead of the hail.

The sky was always almost green before the hail. The color of sickly plants hoping for more sunlight. The color of duckweed being slowly smothered by algae being poisoned by the water it required to live. I hated the color green. That shade of green. I missed waving forests of kelp, the way light gleamed on a passing leatherback turtle, flashes of fish sneaking through a maze of coral. I missed the green of new sea oats as they were sown on the dunes, flip flops kicked off tiny feet and often forgotten. So many types of green. So many vibrant types of green. Nothing like this sickly warning.

Precipitation was almost as bad as the sea itself, though I was not without my defenses. I pulled long sand-and-stone scored legs to my chest, settled my chin on my knees, and pulled my skin around me. Hunched under a span of spotted fur I looked like a stone pitted by hissing, acid-laced rain, the shadows of my posture seemed the result of crushing, poisoned hail. I watched the surf churn, scrabbling at a shoreline so battered it seemed almost cruel, if I could not hear the oceans desperate wailing.

And I wanted nothing more than to scream my own loneliness and pain back in answer. We were two parts of a whole, the sea and I. But there was nothing more than a final comfort to be found in her embrace these days, and I was not that desperate, not even something as old and irrelevant as myself- a selkie unable to swim.

I stared at my mother, hummed in an attempt to hear anything apart from the horrible pounding surf, the pounding of my heart as I yearned to swim. I should have turned inland, joined the few of us that were left in our bid for a bit of sanity and self-preservation. But I could not stand the thought of leaving our mother to suffer alone- poisoned, dying, calling out her fear and agony.

I would have missed them, had I turned inland with my sisters and brothers, had I not been sitting as I always sat, bearing witness to the death of a most ancient thing. I almost did anyway, passed them off as an illusion, a mirage.

But no...I could smell them- salty sweat, salty blood. I could hear their cries over those of my mother. I was standing before I processed the action, poised like a hound on a scent. Humans. At sea. Stupid enough, desperate enough, to be trying a boat. They were being tossed about, clinging desperately to their battered vessel as my mother tried to buck them from her back as would an unbroken horse. They hurt her, cutting through water that was so soiled, so sick, it was a constant source of pain. They hurt her, and she was going to kill them.

It was, admittedly, not my brightest idea. But I had folded my skin around me just before I touched the edge of the surf, felt it burn. This me was made for swimming, for soothing and calming the sea. I sang the quiet songs only selkies know, coaxing, trying for even a moment of calm that would let me get to the boat, let me guide it to shore before the poison killing my mother ate away at my skin.

She heard me, my mother, and paused with a mighty gasp of wind and wave. It was the wavering inhalation that came before an outburst too powerful to be suppressed, I sensed how the waters gathered, how the currents shifted, and did what I could with the magic I had.

Selkies were made for enticing. I bobbed there a moment, just out of reach, brown eyes wide and adoring. Encouraging. I made sure they could see me, I threw every bit of glamor I had to make myself the most appealing thing those humans had ever seen. I sang out the siren calls of my southern sisters- using ithem to coax to safety as opposed to destruction. And the boat turned, slowly cutting through the returning furor of the ocean to follow me to the skeleton of a pier. A safe place for them to cast a rope, to tie, to clamber up and away from the surging riptide. A place for me to guide them out of the sputtering rain and into the old building with its battered but mostly intact roof, ancient soda machines and a game table.

My skin over my shoulders like some manner of primitive cloak they could not help but recognize me- once a seal, now a naked, somewhat scrawny man. A selkie. There was a chance I could be slaughtered for my skin and the protection it offered against the poisoned rain, but they looked too exhausted, too damaged, to offer much of a threat. And they had a wee one. I reached without thinking, taking the baby from his mother's exhausted, rain-burned arms, whispering and conjuring, singing poison ingested from crying in the rain out of his blood. It slithered like tar from the corners of his eyes, tracked down his face like tears until I wiped it away.

"I am Morgan." I was surprised at how clumsy my voice was, unused to the shape of my own name, how round it was, open and inviting. "I saw your boat."

"Thank you. We were..."

"We were fucking terrified." Her mate did not seem to harbor any of the tentative attitude toward me that she did. He ran a hand through the uneven clumps of wet hair that clung to his scalp, wincing a bit as the wetness burned. "Didn't think we would make it to shore, that storm coming out of nowhere like it did. Like they do."

I could taste the storm in the back of my throat, bitter and angry and unwilling to wind down. Male selkies breathed storm winds. Our hearts beat to thunder. But these storms frightened even me. "This is a particularly bad one. I could hear it when it was born, far out over the waves, so unhappy..."

We stood there, again awkwardly aware of things different between us, things of blood and bone. Of seal skins and selkie songs. But we shared a very solid need to be indoors as the wind began to howl and the rain really started to come down. "It isn't much, but this has served as a sort of home to me- I am happy to share it for as long as you need."

"I am Josiah. My wife is Marilyn. Our son is Aaron. Thank you for the shelter."

***

Shelter was easy. Realizing that humans would require bedding and other comforts was hard- I was used to rolling into my skin, curling up seal-stoic against the elements. Had there been another selkie to see me dashing from abandoned human home to abandoned human home, my skin held over my head like nothing more than a strange umbrella I am sure I would have been embarrassed. As it was I pretended to ignore the way Marilyn almost laughed. And she tried to ignore the fact I was not human. But I found blankets that were not too mildewed in what had once been a rather magnificent vacation home, a few changes of clothes that may fit. A set of blocks that had once been used to build sandcastles. The beach was not safe, but Aaron could manipulate them indoors.

I helped them build a nest of human castoffs in the corner of the pier house. My house. I grew used to the way Marilyn sang quietly when it stormed loudest, when she pieced together a meal out of whatever Josiah or I brought in. I grew comfortable with the feel of them around me, never silent, all rustles and breaths and footsteps. They were islanders, originally- holdouts after most of their community had fled, taking their chances atop the poisoned waters as opposed to watching the waves slowly eat away at the land offering them some measure of protection. They had been proud, refusing to leave. But a baby had changed everything and as the waves cut closer with every season they had made the decision to follow the path their community had chosen earlier, active attempt over a passive resignation to their fate.

I enjoyed the shape of their names in conversation- the breathy, bemused resignation of Josiah, the shy exhalation of Marilyn and the broad joy of Aaron. I grew to love the smell of them- salty like the sea never was anymore. The light salt of their sweat was omnipresent, almost soothing, butit caught my attention, my breath, when Marilyn wept one morning. The salt of her tears was so sharp to my nose it hurt. It hurt. I was next to her, brushing each precious bit of salt water off of her face with an intensity I knew frightened her, but I could do nothing to stop myself, even as I licked my fingers clear of her tears, something that had withered long ago deep inside me swelling. I chased after it, song rumbling deep in my chest, a hunters croon. I swept her up in it, my touch as rough as the waters below as I swept her terror away. This was not the slow seduction on a selkie male in the moonlight. This had the hard edge of survival to it. I called to her, to the soft corners of humanity that were so easily edged in salt, and lapped up everything she offered.

"Morgan."

A human male, interrupting. The waters below raged in response to the pounding of my pulse, beating at the ancient pier.

It has been written into every selkie story ever told- we are a tragedy. There are no happy endings with seal wives, to be found in the arms of a seal husband. It is a fine line we straddle between domesticated and savage, we live in that liminal space between sea and shore. And in this battered world that line had been blurred so badly.

His name was lost to me, the human male charging forward to defend his mate. My own was the roar of the surf, the threatening rumble of thunder, a bit of self carefully tucked away under need and want and danger. He should have known better, but humans never do. They cannot sense a threat they cannot overcome on the air the way we can, taste it. They always try, humans. They will always try. It was an altercation that ended in

Josiah broken and bleeding, the smell of salt so strong in the air. I do not remember much more than Marilyn's screaming, the way her tears had bittered so, gone from soothing to burning and the way they brought some strange sort of regret that tasted like bile all through me. I remember the pier giving one final, grateful groan as the acidic poison of the ocean finally won and it was able to start to slide to its rest.

I left the human woman to her mate- their salt was as poisonous to me as the sea now that my need did not overwhelm me so. Bitter with that strange strain of regret that fae beings sometimes get caught up in it would curdle my innards until there was nothing left but a tormented shell. Best leave that salt, best leave that woman. I left the human to mourn her mate and saved her baby.

Agile, unburdened by grief, I took Aaron in my arms and left my home.

I did not watch the final splash of the pier house. I did not take the burden of its death, the deaths of its inhabitants, onto my shoulders. The world was a bit too broken for anyone to take responsibility for events such as this, tragedies such as these. It was not in the nature of a selkie anyway. We mourn, we grieve, but we do not suffer from an overabundance of guilt. That is a human condition. Before the waters went foul, my experience of humanity began and ended with soft smiles and touches in the moonlight- carefully cunning gestures, the slip of skin against skin and soft sounds of surprise and delight. Now it expanded to include the howling of a small body left to become too hungry, too thirsty, too tired, too dirty.

I traveled away from the sea, away from my long vigil at my Mother's deathbed, my attention now on caring for this demanding, disastrously fragile, little creature I had taken responsibility for. He suckled at my fingers as if hoping they would produce more than a sticky sort of mud as saliva mixed with whatever had soiled me most recently. It was difficult to locate creatures to milk, and I fear my little human grew on a rather eclectic diet- meat that was too tired or worn to put up much of a fight, inland plants I had no business determining the edibility of. But grow he did. He grew curious and vocal and gangly and swift. He wanted to know the words for all the things we saw, and some of the things he saw only traces of.

He never thought it strange that I would stop and stare at the sky sometimes, just before the birds would pause in whatever they were doing and then take to frantic wing. He would simply start looking about for someplace safe, some sort of shelter for his vulnerable body. Somewhere to pass the time while it rained and I rolled up in my sealskin and lay nearby. The erratic, vindictive weather was not alien to him. Neither was a selkie.

He gave me back my words, reminding me of the shape and feel of them, the way some of them tickled, some of them hurt. He reminded me of family, of sitting with seal maidens and selkie men on rocky shores and laughing through philosophy and terrible poetry. He taught me how wide the word loneliness could shape through one's spirit, even while a bright young human chittered and chattered an accompaniment to the rain just to the left.

"Aaron." His name was wide in the middle, a smiling shape that opened and closed on a promise and a smirk. He cocked his head at me from where he lay in a nest of leaf mulch, warm with decay, smelling like autumn used to. "Aaron, are you lonely?"

"How?" His sentences were short, clipped and concise as someone far older, as the taciturn selkie that served as parent and friend. "I am not alone."

How to explain the feel of loneliness- the narrow shape of detachment, the slippery fear of drifting? How to explain the taste of loneliness to a human child who did not know schoolyards and malls and choirs and drum circles? How to explain the way it was worms of the spirit, eating away at intangibles until all the parts that mattered were as tattered as old lace?

How to explain the horribly slow death of a selkie away from his family and his sea, how a small human, even one as exceptional as one's current company, could not slow the bleed from this wound?

That was not the talk to have with a child. I huffed, rolling tight into my skin until there was nothing there but a seal to curl close to the boy. Seals have no use for words. Small boys take comfort in contact.

* * *

I don't think I quite noticed when Aaron stopped being small, when it was two men who wandered through stunted woodlands and battered fields in search of water that was safe enough to drink, things that were alive enough to eat. But his voice deepened into a thunderous boom when he laughed, mouth wide, expression uninhibited by the concern of what others might think. He was a wild thing, expressive, uninhibited, curious. He was as close to fae as I have ever seen a human be, and I suppose it should have pleased me, this wonderful child of mine.

He did please me, with his broad smiles full of contentment with a situation I cannot conceive of anyone, anything, else being content with. He coaxed smiles out of me- soft expressions that were so unfamiliar, almost uncomfortable, but ones I enjoyed. Even as we slipped through broken down buildings, stepping over rubble and bits of organic matter we chose not to think too deeply about, or as we trudged through swaths of dead grass, around the edges of swamps that smelled of chemicals more than rot, Aaron shared secrets and smiles with me. Smiles I found myself returning more and more often as time moved on.

I was smiling when they found me, a group of humans far less domesticated than my Aaron. Their bodies scarred and battered with burns, skin hanging to bone out of sheer stubborn determination. So emaciated, so angry. So aware of what I was. I was glad my Aaron was foraging, that we were apart for this time- I did not want him to be hurt. I did not want him to see me hurt them.

For I may be old, missing my family and far past when I would rather be taking my last swim in my Mother, but I am a selkie. The thunder that accompanied the way I bared my teeth would bring Aaron running, the way the clouds gathered through a previously clear sky would have him worried. But the rain was not meant for him. The burning of the rain, the scorching death of the lightning- those were meant for the ones who were after my skin.

"Morgan!"

The humans fought with tooth and nail, the weapons left to them in this battered remnant of the world they remembered, the world they had broken so far past repair. They tore at my flesh, bled me even as my rains burned them and our voices mixed in cried of furious pain that were indistinguishable once uttered. My skin my skin they were going to take my skin... I could feel the rains burn as my skin was pulled to and fro from where I had it over my head and shoulders, down my back.

"Morgan!"

My Aaron, face red and blistered and not at all smiling. He pulled a human from me, not even seeming to care as he snapped its neck with the same practiced ease he had snapped the bones of prey animals we had stumbled across. My Aaron, damaged by my killing rain, and not at all human as he fought to defend the only family he had. So fae, so feral, and for a moment I was horrified at what I had raised.

And then I was honored. Something settled into those worm tortured, lace-holed parts of me, warm and for the first time in so very long content. At the end of a slaughter, bleeding and blistered, as I sang the storms away, I finally curled myself around the concept of family. After so very long, I had family. Aaron looked up at me, blood slipping down one cheek. "Morgan. I found water. Clean water."

Water. My mouth split wide into a smile and I began to laugh.

***

Water. For growing vegetation that could sustain life. For drinking. For swimming. Clean water was the key, the thing that had been missing for so very long. Aaron led me, the both of us limping and leaning on the other, to a system of caves, down deep where plants glowed and fish did not even bother with eyes. Fish. Plants. My pulse battered at my veins with excitement. Anticipation.

There was water indeed. An entire underground lake lit by

bioluminescence. The air was fresh in a way I had never anticipated, so far underground. Clean. The first time a bit of moisture dripped from the unseen ceiling and landed on my cheek I flinched, and then let the sheer wonder of the sensation, the lack of pain, swell within me. I caught a motion in the waters and I shivered, standing still as a hound on point, sensing something that had been missing at the edges of my awareness for so long - there were selkies in the water. I wanted...I wanted with an intensity that was terrifying to join my sisters and brothers. To introduce my son.

My son. Blistered from rain, hanging awkwardly back and watching, waiting to see what I would do. I could watch every emotion chase across his face, I could have tasted it in the one tear tracing down a cheek had I been inclined to sample it like the rare vintage it was. But I did not need to. I understood human's enough. I understood loneliness enough. My Aaron was waiting to see if I was going to slip into that water, a seal, and never slip back out. My Aaron was wondering what it would be like to be an orphan.

Selkies are tragedies. We always have been, always will be. As the world repairs herself we will be down in these caves, in this water, writing new tragedies as humans stumble across us. Aaron was my tragedy. I could still remember the shape of Marilyn's smile, the way Josiah's name stretched and shaped my mouth. Selkies would always be tragedies but, perhaps, for this one time, the tragedy could be my own.

I slipped my skin off my shoulders, stepped back and wrapped my arms around Aaron in a hug, pressing flesh to flesh, burns to burns. I pulled my skin up and around his shoulders, pressing a kiss to his cheek. "Aaron." The shape of his name was a smile, a smirk and a promise at the end. His name was a promise. I wanted to promise him so much. "My Aaron."

I am no selkie maid to lose her skin on a moonlit beach, to remain captive as a human until I win it back. But this thing I would give freely- my skin, my magic. I wrapped it tight around Aaron, watched his eyes go wide and curled close around the new-made harbor seal that stood still and awkward on the stone floor."My little selkie."

I know well the pulse of tides through the blood, the urge to wet every inch of the body and roll weightless in the embrace of a body of water, the pure joy of being. I watched as a human heart stretched to accommodate so much more than it had ever anticipated. My heart would always call to my Mother the sea and that call burned harsh with every breath, but here, as my Aaron felt everything new and the whiskers on his face gave an excited quiver I knew that particular sickness had not slipped into him along with my magic. He could be content deep in the earth, held secure in the arms of a different Mother, submerged in Her secret pools.

I stepped back, wrapped my arms around myself, feeling exposed in a way that had nothing to do with nudity, but strangely comfortable. "Go on. Meet your sisters and brothers. Meet your family." It had never been about me, none of this. It had always been about a small vulnerable baby crying in his mother's arms, so like the crying of a seal pup who had lost sight of its mother. It had always been about one human in the middle of a world that way beyond noticing the little things, beyond caring. I had been beyond caring, and now I was near to bursting with deep contentment. This new selkie, these new selkies- I could taste their newness in the air, could see it in the brightness of their eyes, eyes so unlike mine- they would survive.

How many others had done as I just had? How many human children had cried out, only to be taken up in the arms of seal maids, of selkie men, raised as wild and wonderful things, and finally given that greatest thing a selkie had to give? Selkies were tragedies, salt of the sea and salt of tears. Always wanting something just out of reach, on the next shore. Always reaching.

But this was a new beginning, a bit of a gleam on the horizon. These were new selkies, and they were free to make their own story, their own magic.

I walked away, making my way back out of the caves as Aaron slid into the water, graceful as any selkie born. I left those young and joyous seal folk behind in their glowing cave full of blind fish and crawling things, that cave so full of life. I walked back out into a world that had died so long ago and for once thought not of death but of a potential recovery. The chance was in the gleaming eyes of a small herd of seal folk, in the hope that curled warm through my stomach I walked, finally towards the embrace of my Mother. My mouth shaped words I had wanted to say for so very long, testing the shape of them against the warmth in my stomach, fascinated with how well they fit. "I'm coming home."

About the Authors

Joyce Chng lives in Singapore, writes urban fantasy, science fiction and things in between. Also YA. Also steampunk. Her fiction has appeared in We See A Different Frontier and Crossed Genres. She tweets at @jolantru and howls at A Wolf's Tale (http://awolfstale.wordpress.com).

Nina Waters is the pen name of Claire Houck. Claire has loved writing for as she can remember - her writing "debut" was the epic, "My Little Ponies and the Mean Glob," printed on dot matrix after being at work with her mother for a day in the late 80s. She soon moved from fan fiction (not that she knew that's what she was doing!) onto original writing. Though she has written several short stories and four novel-length manuscripts, this is only her second publication. Claire lives in Schenectady, NY, with her wife, and when she's not writing - sadly, most of the time - she is devoting her energy to opening her own bakery.

K Orion Fray may be from the wine country of New York, but Rion currently lives in the sunny southern part of Virginia. No matter what house they're found in, Rion lives with a couple of cats, their owners, and a slew of apocalypse plans. When not writing, Rion can usually be found narrating audiobooks, voice acting on YouTube, watching movies, running away from the zombies on their phone, or—of course—drinking wine. Rion is also currently enrolled in the Creative Writing MFA program through Carlow University in Pittsburgh, PA. More of Rion's work can be found at http://www.korionfray.com.

A year ago, **E.V. O'Day** graduated from the University of Calgary with an English BA in one hand and a crumpled plan in the other. Using her Creative Writing Concentration as an anchor, she flung herself wholly into the world of dark fantasy where she travels for stories in questionable company. Right now, an isolated bounty hunter and a restless pack of werewolves each vie for her attention. When she isn't writing, E.V. juggles a day job at a building that's burned down twice in the past 100 years, blogs for AnxietyInk.com, reads like a madwoman, meets with the Alberta Romance Writers' Association (ARWA), and strives to find consistent time to complete her first novel.

It's a long way from a rural homestead to an apocalyptic landscape, but Mrs. **Lyn Thorne-Alder** has traveled the distance there and back again enough times to know the route.

Lyn grew up on a steady diet of fantasy and sci-fi: Piers Anthony, Robert A. Heinlein, Mercedes Lackey, as well as movies like Mad Max and Conan the Barbarian. She likes to say "It all began with the winged cat-people": a make-believe scenario inspired by fantasy novels and Voltron cartoons which led to her first-ever novel attempt. Thirty years later, the cat-people are still flying.

From rural to apocalypse and back to rural: Lyn Thorne-Alder currently lives in the Finger Lakes with her husband and a handful of politically-minded cats. An oenophile, bibliophile, and lover of the outdoors, Lyn enjoys gardening, hiking, various crafts, reading and, of course, writing.

M. J. King is a Maine-based fantasy writer. Her short story A Trick of Shadows was published in the Fight Like a Girl anthology. She is part of the Anxiety Ink group blog and an irregular contributor to The Word Count Podcast. You can find Melissa on her personal blog (http://mjkingwrites.wordpress.com) or follow her on Twitter (@mjkingwrites).

Sarah Lyn Eaton is an author, playwright, genealogical researcher, and ritualist. She has recovered the names of over 1,750 members of her family tree, which she peppers into her stories as a means of honoring them, and is a third cousin, six times removed of the poet Thomas Greenleaf Whittier. Sarah Lyn grew up on the Erie Canal near Lake Ontario and currently lives at the confluence of two rivers. Like the dryads in her story, she can't root herself in a landscape without water. Her graphic story "Of Roots and Rings" appears in Elf Love (Pink Narcissus Press, 2010). Her play, Because... Women Were Created to Carry Two Hearts was produced through the Performing Arts Company at SUNY Fredonia. She keeps a weekly blog about her ancestor and genealogy work at walkingwithancestors.blogspot.com.

Kate Larking is a University of Calgary graduate with a degree in Marketing and a minor in English. While keeping on top of the newest digital marketing research, she writes speculative fiction for both YA and adult markets. Residing in Calgary, she is the elected secretary for the Alberta Romance Writers' Association (ARWA) and a member-at-large for the Imaginative Fiction Writers' Association (IFWA).

Ross Bennett is excited to make his debut in this anthology. Strange folklore and apocalypses have always ranked among his favorite topics to read and write on. Most of his work is shared through pen and paper roleplaying, where Ross is collaborating to create a guidebook for the novel world of Ranvier. When not writing, Ross spends as much time as he can learning how and why a person's mind, people, and society work.

By day, **Crystal Sarakas** works in public broadcasting as a news anchor, talk show producer, professional beggar for money, and intern wrangler (which is surprisingly like herding young hipster cats). At night, usually right in the middle parts when she should be sleeping, she's muttering to herself and making up stories. In her spare time, she reads, gardens, and mutters some more. She's a Southerner (from Texas) who has been living in Yankee territory (central New York) for 16 years and is still trying to teach her friends real manners. She's working on a book about dead people, sweet tea, old cemeteries, and the shenanigans that ensue when you mix all three.

Zack Smith is an artist and designer from New York. He is pretty okay at drawing and pretty less okay at writing in the third-person. He can be found at http://zacksmithart.com.

About the Editors

April Steenburgh is an author and freelance editor and eBook formatter. 'What Follows' is the second anthology she has edited. Her short story 'How Much Salt' can be found in 'The Modern Fae's Guide to Surviving Humanity', published by DAW. She is also a reference librarian at a community college and digital literacy librarian at a public library in NY. When not engaging in writerly pursuits, she can be found up to her elbows in dirt in her extensive gardens, geocaching, or firespinning. You can find her at http://aprilsteenburgh.com/.

C. Lennox traded the hustle and bustle of New Orleans for the wilds of the mountains of North Carolina—and by wilds…there are trees outside her door—when she was just a teenager. Since then she has remained close to the mountains, but has not forgotten her roots. She works as a freelance graphic designer, and in her "spare" time indulges in her preferred medium of photography. She spends her post-graduate life annoying her cats, hiking with the dog and enjoying the fact that she can watch television and read fiction again.

Her first collaborative anthology as editor was *Fight Like a Girl: A Short Story Anthology*, published last year.